MELT

ELE FOUNTAIN

PUSHKIN CHILDREN'S

Pushkin Press
71–75 Shelton Street
London WC2H 9JQ

Melt was first published by Pushkin Press in 2021

1 3 5 7 9 8 6 4 2

ISBN 13: 978-1-78269-288-1

Designed and typeset by Tetragon, London
Printed and bound by CPI Group (UK) Ltd, Croydon, CR0 4YY

www.pushkinpress.com

Contents

AFTER

For Mum and Dad

We borrow the earth
from our children

CHIEF SI'AHL

Storm

A low sound hums across the frozen air. In the distance, four dark shapes glide through the white, like ghosts in negative. Their headlights cast a yellow glow. The only colour in a land of white and grey. When the snow is deep, the humming sound is lower. When there are ridges to cross, it is more like an angry wasp. On each snowmobile sits a figure, dressed in layers of leather and fur. A man leads the group, followed by a woman, then a woman, followed by a man.

They have been travelling since first light. Soon they must find a sheltered place to spend the night. This far north the sun barely rises above the horizon before sinking once more to slumber. They know where they are going. These trails were used by their parents; by their grandparents; by generations before them all.

Wind whistles over the tundra. Everything in its path must bow down or drift. Nothing is foolish enough to challenge the wind, not this far north. The place where

11

they are heading is protected from its relentless power. A small wooden hut nestled in a hollow. Normally they would be there by now. Lighting the fat-lamp to dry their sealskin mittens. But the weather has surprised them. At this time of year it is very cold but calm. A good time to hunt caribou. The weather was calm and still when they left, now it is the opposite. A gale is blowing in from the sea.

The two shapes at the back begin to fall behind. The man's snowmobile is losing power. The woman slows down to wait for him. He needs to check the cylinders but it's not possible here. When they reach shelter he will check. For now, they will just have to keep going, however slowly.

The wind is getting stronger by the minute. A flurry of snow whips past. More snow falls, and the wind blows it into smoky swirls. The two lead vehicles fade to pale grey, then seconds later disappear from view. They will arrive at the shelter first and get things ready for the others.

The man's snowmobile slows and then stops. He tries to restart it but the engine is dead. He will have to leave it here. It is a hard decision. They will fix it or drag it home on their return journey. The woman motions to the man. He climbs on the back of her snowmobile. The fur around the edge of their hoods captures flakes of snow for a split second before the wind blasts it away. The pair start moving, but the blizzard is becoming a white-out.

After five minutes they are forced to stop again, disorientated. There is no faint glow from the sun to show them which way to head. The landmarks they have memorized, which their ancestors memorized, have disappeared. They cannot get off the snowmobile. The wind would be too strong for them to stand up. The man leans forwards and hugs the woman. His arms barely reach round the many layers she is wearing.

Darkness is falling. They cannot stay here. They will certainly freeze to death. They must keep going. This land is part of them, they breathe its rhythms, but those rhythms are becoming unpredictable. There shouldn't be a storm now. It shouldn't blow in this suddenly, and with such force. The weather is changing, and centuries of knowledge cannot keep up. The bonds which connect people and nature are beginning to fray. Something precious beyond imagining, is coming apart.

Yutu 1

Someone shoves me hard from behind. I stumble to my knees and my school bag flies a few metres to the right. A strong hand grips my shoulder and tries to roll me over. I look up. Sami stares down at me. I grab his coat and pull him into the snow next to me. We roll over like seals. Four or five kids stand and watch, shouting for Sami to get me, hold me down. After one final twist I roll him onto his side and sit on him. He can't move. The snow in my ear melts and runs inside my hood and down my neck. I stand up and brush the snow from my legs and arms, then offer Sami my hand.

'Nice try,' I say.

'Nearly had you,' he grins back. 'So nearly.'

I collect my bag from the snowy edge of the path and give it a shake.

'Come round tomorrow? Gaming?' he asks.

'I have to check first. Grandma might need something doing.'

'You're going to start your assignment, aren't you?' Sami says. 'You're such a nerd.'

I smile. We both know he's right.

Sami and the others head off down the path towards a cluster of small houses. 'See ya!' they call without turning round. Sami waves a hand in the air.

I walk slowly in the opposite direction, towards a low hill, dyed orange by the setting sun. At the foot of the hill is a building unlike any others in our village. The other houses have smooth dark-red walls and look as if they are floating. They need to be raised up on pillars, or else the heat from inside would melt the solid permafrost foundations, and the buildings would sink. This house looks as if it has already sunk beneath the earth and then risen up to breathe, like some kind of rocky whale. Its walls are made of rough stones the size of someone's head. They pile up to join a wooden roof which looks like it was made from driftwood. Because it was.

This is my house. I live here with my *anaanat-siaq*—my grandma. She's always lived here. People keep trying to move her into what she calls *modern* houses, even though families have been living in these *modern* houses since well before I was born. They worry our house isn't warm enough, that without pillars it might begin to sink. I could tell them it never gets warm enough in our house to melt any kind of frost, let alone permafrost. Often I can see my own breath. I'm used to it though. The raised sleeping area at the back is always cosy, which helps.

I bend down to open the front door—also made from driftwood. The doorway is Hobbit-height, which was fine until recently. Now I am officially the tallest boy in my class, possibly in my school. I bang my head on the doorway at least once a day.

Inside, Grandma is sitting in her chair, sewing. A piece of sealskin is draped across her knees, colourful stiches blooming along one edge. She looks up and gives me a smile.

'Welcome home,' she says, as if I've been away for days.

I dump my bag on the floor and sit in the chair next to her. I don't know how she can see well enough to sew. Weak sunlight filters through the window behind her. I switch on the light and she makes a soft sighing sound. She doesn't like the light. She only stopped using her seal-fat lamp a few years ago. I had a cough which wouldn't get better. In the end the doctor said the lamp had to go. It kept turning the walls black anyway.

'How was school?' She speaks to me in the language of our ancestors. She knows English words, but it tires her out to make the strange noises English requires. The old language starts at the back of the throat. The sounds are shorter and more precise. Very different to English sounds. I love the rhythm of her words, calm and steady.

'School was OK. I have homework and a science assignment to finish over the holidays. I don't know if anyone else will bother doing them.'

Grandma is silent. She looks at me, her hands resting on the sealskin. Grandma speaks when she has thought things through. Never in anger, or impulsively. That means conversations often move quite slowly. On a few occasions I've begun to wonder whether she's fallen asleep, then quietly and carefully she will begin to talk.

'What will you do to have fun, this holiday?' she asks, finally.

'I don't know. I'll think about that when I've done the assignment. Maybe play table tennis with Sami. Or some ball hockey.'

She looks at me. She looks past the words and studies my face. I swear she can see right inside my head.

Perhaps it's time to tell her what I really want. I have a feeling she already knows. The idea has been floating round my brain for months. The more I think about it, the faster my words evaporate. The opposite of Grandma, I guess.

'If the weather is good, maybe I could go north to the cabin for a few days.'

Grandma makes another soft sighing sound.

I can't stop now.

'I want to take the sledge. Petur has said he'll let me borrow two dogs. You're always telling me it's important to keep the old ways alive.'

'Learning the old ways is one thing. Taking the sledge because we don't have a snowmobile is a different thing. You're too young to go off on your own. Especially with someone else's dogs.'

I feel my shoulders sink. Grandma has a way of saying things which makes it hard to argue. I try a different tack.

'I want to bring back some seal meat. I want to contribute to the communal food store. I know the store is running low.'

After a few minutes she says, 'When I was young, boys would go out to watch seal hunts as soon as they could walk on the sea ice. They would learn how to find a lair, how to find a blowhole. How to throw a harpoon. It would take years to learn everything. Then they would be ready to hunt for themselves.'

'But I've been out with Petur loads of times. He's been teaching me for *years*. He says I have a gift for hunting.'

Grandma stares at me for a long time. 'You cannot go alone,' she says. End of story. She doesn't say that, but it's clear.

I pick up my school bag and head to the back of the house. 'I'm going to read for a bit,' I call.

I lie on my bed and stare at the ceiling, made up of close-fitting wooden panels. The walls are clad in the same honey-coloured wood. Each piece is different. Some have swirling knots, or wavy lines. I know them all. Beneath me, the bedcover is made of caribou skin. Sewn together by Grandma. People come from other villages to buy things she has made. People respect her because she is a village elder, but also because she makes beautiful things, using techniques which are slowly being forgotten. They also respect her because she looks after me.

For seven years Grandma has taken care of me, even though she barely makes enough money to pay for the oil which lights the stove. Maybe that's why I find it so hard when we disagree. But I don't think she's realized that I'm not a little boy any more. I'm fourteen. I can't stay in this frozen village for ever. She wants me to learn the old ways, but she won't let me go and try them out for real. She doesn't like using the food store, but she won't let me go and hunt. We seem to be pulling in opposite directions more and more, and I don't know how to fix it.

I guess there's one thing I can rely on. It's Friday and that means trout for dinner. Again.

Bea 1

I walk through the school gates. My stomach gives a little flutter. I so thought I was over caring about new schools. This is my fifth in five years. New school, new town, new country. Same me. I keep my head down and walk to the main entrance. Mum asked if she should come with me, but then everyone in the whole school knows you're the new kid on your first day. Not just everyone in your class. I push past the entrance door and walk up to reception. A lady with straight brown hair and glasses glances up from whatever she is doing. The faintest look of surprise flits across her face, then she takes in my brand-new uniform and probably nervous expression and says, 'Is today your first day?'

She's good.

'Yes. I'm supposed to be in Miss Stewart's form group. Ninth grade.'

She smiles brightly. 'Well, at least you've come

prepared. Wait here,' she says, like there's somewhere else I might be rushing off to.

There are three grey seats pushed against the wall. I sit in the one furthest from the door. Never sit in the middle seat and risk being sandwiched between two people you don't want to talk to. The end seat at least limits it to one.

A bell sounds. Seconds later the entrance door slams open and kids pour in, talking and laughing. Some of them stare at me. Mostly girls. No one smiles.

Five minutes later, someone comes to fetch me. My 'buddy'. My buddy has a pixie haircut, only advisable for those with exceptional cheekbone structure, which she has. She speaks to the receptionist, then turns to look at me. I can tell one thing instantly. She doesn't want to be my buddy.

'I'm Stella,' she says, walking briskly down the corridors so that I have no hope of remembering my way. 'It means star in Italian.'

'*Da quale galassia sei?*'

'What?' she snaps.

'I was just saying "that's nice". In Italian.'

She gives me a look which means I should not speak until spoken to, and then definitely not in Italian.

'My name's Bea,' I say. 'It means happiness in Latin.'

24

'I'm a prefect, and class representative,' she says, as if that settles everything. 'If you have any questions during your first week, you're to ask me.'

She stops abruptly halfway down a corridor, and knocks on a classroom door, then pushes me in front of her so that I receive the full laser-beam treatment from thirty pairs of curious eyes.

'Welcome, Beatrice,' the teacher says, smiling warmly. 'I'm Miss Stewart. Please take any free seat and I'll come round with your timetable in a minute.'

I look around for a free seat. There's one at the back, and one at the front. I choose the one in the front row, next to a girl with long brown hair.

As soon as I'm settled, the girl whispers, 'That's Jessica's seat.' I turn my head to look at her, confused. 'She's sick today. You'll have to sit somewhere else tomorrow.'

'I'm Bea,' I say. 'Are you feeling OK? You look a little pale. Maybe you've caught what Jessica has.'

The girl with long brown hair frowns at me. She opens her pencil case and turns it gently from side to side. Light flashes off a small mirror which she is peering into while pretending to look for a pen.

I follow the 'star' to my first two lessons. She shows me where the toilets and lockers are.

At lunchtime, she reluctantly escorts me to the

cafeteria. I am starving. My stomach's getting used to a new time zone. Normally I'd have had lunch six hours ago. I choose the biggest-looking option and scan the dining hall for an empty table. Scanning for empty chairs and tables is one of my special skills. I spot one right at the back.

'This way,' Stella instructs, before I can make a break for freedom. She chooses the table where brown-hair girl, whom I now know is called Becky, is sitting. Three more girls join us. They alternate between whispering to each other and staring at me. I start to eat my food. Someone giggles, then stops abruptly, like they're trying to exercise self-control in difficult circumstances.

The tall blonde girl sitting opposite me clears her throat dramatically and says, 'You're Bea, right?'

'Yes,' I reply through a mouthful of food. I'm glad we're starting with the easy questions.

'And Bea means... a type of insect?' There are more stifled giggles. The Star remains silent.

'It means joy, in Latin,' I say, keeping eye-contact with the tall blonde girl. I also keep shovelling food into my mouth. There's no need for this to last any longer than absolutely necessary.

'Oh,' she says, in a pretend-interested voice, 'and where do you come from to speak Latin?'

'It's a dead language,' I say. 'No one speaks it.'

Blonde-girl is out of her depth.

'That's so sad,' she says, making a pretend-sad face. 'Well, at least you have us to talk to now. You won't be on your own.'

I finish my last mouthful. 'Thank you,' I say, pushing my chair back. 'One good turn deserves another. I think I saw someone sneeze all over the salad.'

Blonde girl looks down at the lettuce she has just started to eat.

As I walk away a soft buzzing noise comes from their table, getting louder quickly so that people turn to look. Followed by more giggling.

After period four I'm exhausted. I can't face trying to make more polite conversation about why I've started school halfway through the term. I make a bold decision to flee the Star and leave unaccompanied. I somehow remember the way to the lockers. Mine is at the bottom, which is annoying because people bump into you when you're crouching down to open the door. I give up trying to fit my key in the lock and join the flow of people heading for the exit.

I pass through the open doors and shiver. Even though it's spring the weather is freezing. Just when the day can't get much worse, I see that Mum is waiting for me in the car, almost directly outside the school gates. She winds down the window and waves a hand. Her nails are bright red. Whichever country we move to, Mum finds the manicurist before she's even worked out where to buy food.

'Hello, Bea, darling,' she calls through the open window.

By some miracle no one from my class is around to witness this spectacle. I climb into the passenger seat and dump my bag on the floor.

'Good day?' asks Mum, pulling away from the curb.

'Not bad,' I lie.

'I knew you'd like this school. It has an excellent reputation,' she says. When I don't say anything, she adds, 'Did you make any new friends today?'

'Not really.'

'You know you have to make an effort if you're going to make new friends. It doesn't happen without a bit of work.'

I don't have the energy to say, 'And then when I have made new friends, we move countries again.'

'Yes, Mum, you're right.'

'Don't just agree with me, Beatrice, I want to know that you've listened. This is to make things easier for you not me.'

'I have some reading to do for school,' I say, reaching in my bag for a book.

'There are some really nice shops in town. Perhaps we could go there together at the weekend. I saw a lovely little café, too.'

'Sounds good,' I say, opening my Spanish book. 'Sorry, Mum. I've got loads to catch up on.'

'OK, darling.' Schoolwork is pretty much the only sanctioned excuse for silence, with Mum.

I hear a key in the door and shove Hester off my lap. She gives a high-pitched *miaow* of annoyance.

'Hello,' Dad calls. 'Anyone alive?'

I run down the stairs to give him a hug.

'How was your day?' he asks.

I look at the floor and am horrified to realize my eyes are filling with tears. 'It was OK,' I say, wiping my eyes while he takes off his coat.

'Well,' he says, 'I just can't compete with that.'

I laugh and then sniff. Mum clatters about in the kitchen with dinner things.

He sits on the stairs to take off his shoes. 'The company says my reconnaissance plane is ready. I can go down to the airport any time to give it a test flight.' He looks up. 'Shall we go this weekend? I think maybe we'll both need a little time in the clouds.'

'Yes!' I smile for the first time today. 'What about Mum?'

'I'm sure she won't want me to take my first flight in a new plane unaccompanied,' he says. He knows I don't mean, 'Would she like to come?', rather, 'Will she let me go?'

Dad is a model of calm logic with Mum. I can manage the logic. I'm not so good at the calm. Especially when Mum starts talking about *unnecessary risk* and *suitable pastimes*.

He removes his other shoe then sits up straight. 'You know, after this job, we won't have to move around any more. They're paying me so much money that I'll just be able to eat chips and read crime novels for the rest of my life. You can choose where.'

'Do you mean chips or crisps? You know they call crisps chips here?'

'Nobody tells me anything. I mean the hot ones that you sometimes eat with fish. Anyway, I know it's been hard for you, moving around so much. This is it. I promise you.' He holds out his little finger.

'No one does that any more,' I laugh, but I hold out my little finger anyway.

You can't break a pinkie promise.

Yutu 2

The next morning, I am up early. Grandma is busy by the stove, heating her favourite brew. The bittersweet smell of cloudberry-leaf tea drifts around the room. Our kitchen is also our sitting room. Like everything in our house, it's mostly covered in wood panelling or caribou skin.

'Breakfast,' Grandma announces, smiling. She passes me a plate with a thick chunk of bannock bread and a spoonful of berries mixed in fat—sweet and creamy.

'Today I will go to the food store. See what they have,' she says.

'Want me to come?' I ask, my mouth half-filled with bread.

Grandma smiles. 'You're good. Always helping. No need today, though. It's the first day of your holiday.'

What she means is, don't study today.

'Petur is waiting to teach you bone carving. It's a good way to make money,' she says. Grandma is always

31

trying to make me learn bone carving. Bone carving or drumming. I'm quite interested in the drumming, but I know that it wouldn't end there. Next Grandma will want me to dress up in traditional costume and drum whenever there's some kind of ceremony. Even bone carving would be better than that.

'I have plans today,' I say.

Grandma makes her soft sighing sound.

I head to my room and grab my school stuff, then a chunk of bannock bread from the stove.

'See you later, Grandma,' I say, remembering to duck under the doorframe as I leave. There are times when Grandma being slow to answer works in my favour.

I walk down the hill past scattered houses, perched above the snow. The sky is blue with only a few thin clouds on the horizon. Sunlight sparkles on the sea ice. I head towards a large grey building in the centre of the village. The community library. It's always warm in there and I can use community electricity to power my laptop. None of my friends will be up for hours. I open the laptop which took Grandma a year to save up for and try to focus on why I'm doing this, instead of lying in my warm bed. I have to get good grades for university. Better than good. Then I can study in a city somewhere. Somewhere far away, with stuff to do and jobs which don't involve bone carving. I want a different future to the one Grandma has in mind.

Three hours later I have finished the bannock bread and am staring out of the window when a snowball thuds against the glass, quickly followed by another. I stand up and look down to the courtyard. Sami is outside with Jack and Adam. He raises his hands and shrugs—I think in disgust. It seems no one in this place wants me to study. I've had enough anyway. I stuff everything in my bag and head out to join them.

'Come on, nerd. Time to go,' he calls as I walk down the steps.

'Whose house?' I call back.

'Mine,' says Jack. 'I have a new game. Arrived yesterday and I already made it to level three. Beyond level three is impossible.'

'I bet Adam can do it,' says Sami.

'Adam had better not get to level four before I have,' says Jack, as if they're not walking alongside each other.

When I finally go home, the sun has set.

Grandma looks up from the pair of mittens she's sewing. While I take off my boots, she carries on looking, deciding what kind of day I have had.

'Only fish at the store,' she says, 'no caribou. Not much seal either.' She closes her eyes for a second. When she opens them again, she looks sad. 'Every year there are fewer caribou to hunt. We've never run out before.'

'Petur says the seals go to the bay further north,' I say.

'Maybe the Sea Mother is angry. Perhaps we need to make her happy again.'

'Petur says it's because it's too warm in our bay now. Climate change is why they go to the one further up.'

Grandma shakes her head. 'There have always been seals in this bay. Our ancestors hunted seals in this bay. They hunted caribou from the land. Now they are both disappearing. Soon we will have only fish. What if the snow and ice disappear too? Then what are we? Everything that made us who we are, will be gone.'

I've never seen Grandma upset like this before. Then I remember. It's early spring. A good time to track caribou. The days are calm and cold. Like the weekend my parents went hunting with friends. A freak storm blew in. The friends made it back to the village a few days later when it had passed. My parents never came back. That was seven years ago.

I remember being told they had gone. Sometimes, when I've had a bad day, there is an echo of that feeling, deep inside me. A loneliness which won't go away. An ache. I can't really remember life before Grandma though. It feels like a separate place and time. A separate me.

I don't think that's how Grandma sees it. She lost her daughter. Now that I'm older I think she is worried about losing me. Every time there is unseasonal weather, or the hunting is poor she sees it as a sign. A sign to keep me closer. The weather is more frequently weird, and the hunting poor, so perhaps she will never allow me to leave this village. Unless I show her that I can look after myself, that nothing bad is going to happen.

'I'll make some tea,' I say. While I wait for the kettle to whistle, I think about the cabin. I've been there with Petur. I'm ready to go on my own. I think about arriving at Grandma's house dragging two fat seals behind me. I picture her face. At first she will give me one of her 'you should have known better' looks. Then she will smile. A broad smile which makes little creases around her eyes and cheeks.

I pass Grandma her cup, then sit next to her while she picks up another pair of mittens to sew. We often sit this way, in silence. I like it. Inside, though, my thoughts are fizzing like water in a frying pan.

I've made up my mind. I am going to the cabin. Just me.

Bea 2

Something soft pats my hand. I open my eyes and look over at my clock.

'Hester, go away. It's six a.m.' Maybe cats need to adjust to time zones too. I hear the soft crumple of fabric as she jumps up onto my bed. 'Just because I named you after Lady Hester Stanhope, doesn't mean you have to climb everything. Especially on Saturdays.' She turns a few circles before lying down next to me. Purring loudly. She's not the only one who's glad it's the weekend.

I lie with my eyes open, going over my first week at school. Macaroni cheese is the best thing on the menu by a long way. The teachers aren't disappointed with me—yet. Stella is no longer my official buddy. My free trial period has ended, and I don't think she wants to be my unofficial buddy either, which is fine. I'm not interested in making friends and that seems to suit everybody.

I hear noises from downstairs. Dad is up, opening all the kitchen cupboards. Every time we move, it takes ages to learn where things are. Mum seems irritated if we fail to locate anything by the second cupboard, which is unfair. She only knows because she unpacks it all.

I slide out of bed, leaving Hester stretched out on the duvet. She can laze around dreaming catty dreams. She doesn't have a plane to fly.

In the kitchen Dad is making his version of sandwiches, which is like everyone else's but with twice the filling, most of it hanging out.

He doesn't look up. 'Pass the butter, please, Wing Commander.'

'Daaad.'

'I think you mean, sir.'

'Whatever. Here's the butter.' On my third attempt I find the cereal, then hunt for a bowl. 'How long till we leave?'

'Fifteen minutes. OK with you?'

'Aye, Captain.'

'Group Captain, please. We're Air Force, not Navy. Or pirates.'

'And to think I was looking forward to this.'

Mum appears, looking sleepy. 'The weather looks good. I think you'll have a lovely day.'

I feel a twinge of guilt. She wanted to go into town with me today. I guess the weather doesn't need to be good for that. We can go any time.

'I'll take some pictures,' I say.

'Make sure you have plenty of warm clothes, too.'

'I might even wear the thermals you bought me,' I say. I know this will make Mum happy. Usually when she buys me clothes it's a disaster. We have such different taste. Clothes which I can wear underneath other clothes are infinitely less risky.

Ten minutes later I am waiting by the front door. Dad appears with a large rucksack dangling from one hand, mobile phone in the other.

'Ready?' I nod. 'Bye, darling!' he shouts just as my mum appears right behind him.

'Keep an eye on the weather,' she warns, even though the forecast is perfect.

I feel my heart beat a little faster as we pull off the main road. The airport looks small. I can see only five or six planes parked on the tarmac beyond the terminal building. There's also a huge aircraft hangar. I guess it gets pretty snowy here in winter. I'm not sure how you'd go about de-icing an aeroplane before take-off. De-icing a car seems annoying enough.

As soon as we enter the terminal, a man springs

up from a bank of leather chairs beyond a smooth marble floor. The airport might be small, but I sense the people who use it must be doing OK.

'Good morning, Mr Gill.' He smiles a big warm smile. 'And this must be Beatrice,' he says, in a tone which suggests I have earned top marks just by being me. 'Will your wife be joining us?'

'Not today,' Dad says. 'Perhaps next time.'

We both know this isn't true, but Dad is using his Work Voice, so I don't mention it.

'Your plane is refuelled and ready to fly. Please follow me.'

We follow the man to a reception area, where Dad has to sign something, then we head outside. The sky is a cloudless pale blue. Bright morning sunshine reflects off the windows of the stationary aircraft, making me squint. The man leads us to a silver-grey plane with a deep red tick design on the side. It is the shiniest plane I've ever seen.

'This will be yours to use whenever you need it,' the man smiles at Dad. 'Here's the key. On behalf of the company directors, I hope you enjoy your first flight on one of our planes.'

'Thanks,' Dad says.

'Thank you,' I add when the man aims the big flashy grin at me.

He is friendly, but ever-so-slightly creepy. I'm relieved when he heads towards the terminal building. He turns and waves. I wave back, feeling as if he can read my thoughts.

Dad and I climb into the cockpit. Me, Dad and an aeroplane. My perfect Saturday.

'OK, let's run through the preflight checks together,' Dad says.

'Fuel pump is primed, propeller area clear.' I tick things off the list in my head, one by one.

'One-two-eight-delta-foxtrot, you are cleared for take-off, no delays,' a crackly voice comes through on the radio.

'That's us,' says Dad. We taxi slowly to the end of the runway. 'What speed do I need before take-off?'

'Seventy knots,' I answer without thinking.

Dad puts his hand on the side stick and we start to move, accelerating along the white line in the middle of the runway. He pulls the stick back and I feel my stomach rise as we leave the ground.

'Pitch is ten,' says Dad, 'is that OK?'

'Yes. Flaps lowered.'

As we climb, houses become a patchwork of yellowish-red squares. The horizon stretches out on either side. The plane responds gently to each tiny change in pressure or wind speed. I feel connected to the wind, to the air. Peaceful. Small planes are so different to massive jets, where you have no control and no proper view of the skies around you.

'Look,' I say, 'straight ahead.'

Rising up in the distance is a low range of mountain peaks, covered in snow. The land beyond them is white.

'It won't begin to thaw up there for another month at least. If we head north-east and keep going, we might reach the North Pole in time for breakfast tomorrow.'

'Wouldn't we run out of fuel first?'

'Yes. You'd need to refuel somewhere. Probably sensible to wear some warmer clothes too.'

'Where will you be doing your surveys for work?'

'Closer to home. I need to do a few aerial surveys, but mostly seismic.'

Dad is a geologist, or I should say *the* geologist. Every oil company wants to get their hands on him. He finds the biggest reservoirs and the easiest extraction routes. Mum says they like him because he has good instincts. Good instincts save oil companies money, and money is what they like, even more than oil.

'It's extra-tricky when companies want to drill near towns and cities. People like to use petrol and oil, but they don't want to see big refineries or put up with the noise and smell they make. They prefer it to happen somewhere else.'

'Why don't they drill up there then?' I say, pointing to the big white expanse of nothingness ahead.

'Everybody wants to,' he says, 'but it's one of the last wildernesses on our planet. We can't.'

'I didn't think oil companies cared about wildernesses.'

Dad frowns. 'They're businesses. If there's a demand for what they sell, they look for more of it.'

I feel as if I've said the wrong thing.

'Are you ready to take the controls?' I glance at Dad. He is looking straight ahead, but a smile lifts the corners of his mouth. 'Just steer us to the right and then straighten up, then same again in the other direction.'

Excitement fizzes in my chest. 'Now?' I ask.

'Yes, now,' he says calmly.

My palms feel damp as I reach out for the co-pilot side stick, even though Dad says I know enough to get a pilot's licence.

'Over to you,' he confirms.

I gently push the stick to the right and the plane responds, gliding towards the low sun. I tilt the stick back and we straighten up, then I push the stick gently to the left. Our manoeuvres might seem strange to someone watching from the ground. Up here, it feels like freedom. There are no road signs or boundaries. Just sky.

'You're a natural,' Dad says. 'I'm going to take control, now, Wing Commander. We should head back. I don't want to burn up too much fuel on our first trip. They might change their minds about letting us use the plane.'

'OK,' I say. I don't even mention the Wing Commander comment. Right now, I am glowing.

'Probably best not to tell Mum I let you fly the plane,' Dad says.

Yutu 3

'Why?' Sami looks at me with genuine wonder. 'Why would you go and stay in a wooden cabin for a night? You could just sleep outside your front door. I'm sure that would be pretty similar. Except when you wake up you could go inside somewhere warm and have breakfast.'

'I dunno,' I say. 'Maybe Grandma won't worry about me so much if I show her I can look after myself.'

'I think that's a great way to make her worry a whole lot more,' Sami says.

'Also, our house isn't that warm,' I add.

'Sounds like you've made your mind up,' Sami says. 'Anything you need?'

'Well—' I pause. Sami stops setting up the games console to look at me. 'Can I borrow your snowmobile?'

He tilts his head to one side. 'So nothing much! How would I explain a missing snowmobile to my mum?'

'It would only be for one night. You could stay over at Tom's. Your mum will just assume the snowmobile is there with you.'

Tom lives right on the edge of town. No one can be bothered to walk there. Except me.

'You've got this all planned, haven't you?' I smile.

'Anything else?' he asks jokingly.

'Can I borrow your stove?'

'How about I just give you everything I own?'

'Just the stove and your snowmobile would be great.'

'OK,' Sami nods. 'No worries. I'll make sure they both have fuel.'

'You know I can't give you any—'

'Forget it.' Sami raises his hand to cut me off, but he looks like he's about to stop some traffic. 'I don't want money. I'll just tell Mum that I've burnt loads of fuel racing Jack on the flats. She'll be grumpy, but she'll get over it.'

'Thanks, Sami.'

Someone hammers on the front door. Sami leaps up. 'Why can't Jack just knock like a normal person?'

'Just between me and you, right?' I call after him.

'Yeah,' he calls back.

I pick up one of the games controls. I like hanging out with Sami, but I hate gaming. I've never actually said those words to Sami, but he knows it. Today feels different though. I'm looking forward to being the perpetual noob with the lowest KDR. Maybe because it no longer feels like I might be doing this for my whole life. The rest of the world feels one step closer.

I hear the unzipping and unbuttoning of snow-gear. Then a large figure appears in the doorway, hair sticking up in all directions.

'Yutu! Is the library shut?' Jack laughs at his own joke.

'Hey. I went this morning.'

'I hope you're ready to be blown up many times,' he says, coming to join me on the sofa.

'I've been practising.'

'Yeah?'

'I just read the booklet that came with this game,' I say, holding up the instructions.

Jack rolls his eyes. 'You've got to practise for at least six hours a day if you want to become a professional gamer. That time does not include reading the booklet. Then you can start earning money without ever having to leave your house.'

Sami walks in, holding cups and a bottle of something orange and fizzy. 'Everyone wants to go pro. There's so much competition. You have to be really good to make any money.'

'I am really good,' says Jack, sounding annoyed.

'Maybe we need a tournament,' I say. 'Let's see who can wipe me out the fastest in three different games.'

'Yes!' says Sami.

'OK. That won't take long,' Jack nods, but he looks pleased.

'Hi, Grandma,' I say to her back, as she pokes at something on the stove. The rich smell of seal soup fills the house. I realize I didn't have any lunch.

'Where did you go?' she asks.

'I've been at Sami's house.'

She makes a short sound, a little like 'ah'. She's pleased.

Sometimes I wonder if she realizes that all we ever do at Sami's house is play computer games. Maybe she doesn't care, as long as I'm not studying on my own. Perhaps I won't mention that I spent the morning in the library.

'Can I help?' I ask.

'No, it's ready,' she says, turning around to pass me a large steaming bowl. I sit in one of the armchairs. Grandma perches on the edge of hers. She prefers to sit on the floor to eat, but recently she finds it hard to get up again. Floor suits her better.

I start eating, but Grandma is preoccupied. Her eyes glazed. She seems to have forgotten the bowl resting on her lap.

Then she says, 'Did I tell you the story about when you were little?'

I begin to nod, then stop when I realize what she's said. Grandma tells me stories all the time, about the Sea Goddess, the gull-maiden, about the sightless boy and the whale and many others. These stories are part of me. The same stories every child hears before they even understand the words. Each re-telling a little different. Grandma never tells me stories about *me*, though. About when I was little. About things which really happened. I wait impatiently for her to start. But no one rushes Grandma.

Steam rises up from the soup and snakes around her face. Another minute passes, then slowly, quietly, she begins.

'You were always taller than your friends. People said you would be strong. You used to pick up your father's harpoon when you were only just able to walk.' The hand holding my spoon has paused, halfway to my bowl. I lower it slowly, hanging on every word. 'You always wanted to do everything your parents did. You weren't scared of anything, except the dogs which pulled the sledges. Which was

49

surprising, because there were always dogs around, but you were wary of them. One day in summer, your father was going to fish. I remember it was a warm day. There were black swarms of flies around. We walked together to the shore. On the way back home, we saw a boy teasing a *qimmiq* pup. He was pretending to offer it food, then hitting it with a stick when it came towards him. You waited for a minute, then walked towards the boy and the dog. You picked up a stick and we thought you were going to hit the dog too. But you raised the stick to the boy and waved it in his face. He ran away. Then you sat next to the dog and stroked it. Your mother said that was truly brave. The dog wasn't big, nor was the boy. It was truly brave because she knew that you were scared, but that didn't stop you. When your father came home, she told him what had happened. He said that it was good you were brave, because standing up for things when you feel they are right is not always easy. He said life might be hard for you sometimes.'

Grandma looks over at me. I blink away the steam. The aching feeling has crept up on me. I long to see my parents so intensely, to speak to them about that day, I wonder if they might just rise out of the steam in front of me. Maybe that's why Grandma doesn't talk to me about these things. I'm glad she has though. I wonder why she chose now. Glowing somewhere inside the sadness, is something precious. They were proud of me.

Grandma eats in silence. She is leaving me with my thoughts.

'Did your parents always live in this bay?' I ask.

Grandma raises her eyebrows. 'No. Me neither.'

'What? I thought you'd lived in this house all your life?'

'The house was here. We didn't always live in it,' Grandma says. 'We moved around depending on the season. Near the lakes in summer, near the sea ice in winter. We'd live in a snow house, or a tent made from animal skins. Other times we would be here.'

I knew that my ancestors used to live like that. I'd just never realized Grandma had. That way of life wasn't so long ago after all. I pick up Grandma's bowl and take it over to the sink to wash.

I think about the cabin. About how Mum and Dad used to stay there on hunting trips. Those trips seemed like an enormous adventure to me, but Grandma would go away for months at a time, moving for the best hunting, the best weather. It makes me more desperate than ever to prove that I can do it too.

51

'Grandma, Sami is staying over at Tom's tomorrow night. Do you mind if I stay over too?'

'You go and have fun,' she says without pause for thought. 'I need to make a pair of *kamak*.'

Before I wash my bowl, I remove the pieces of seal meat which I put to one side. Later I will add them to the small store I've been collecting in a plastic box outside the back of the house. No one needs a freezer here for at least half the year.

Nearly everything is ready. I just need tomorrow to hurry up and arrive before Grandma asks any questions.

Bea 3

On Monday I decide to walk to school. I've had a week to learn the route and it's not far. It also reduces the risk of Mum-embarrassment.

The bell rings seconds after I walk through the school gate. I flow through reception with the tide of students and glance at the three grey seats by the wall. Last Monday already seems a lifetime ago. When I enter the form room, no one pays me any attention. I look around at the other kids, smiling and sharing stories about the weekend.

I hear laughter behind me. It sounds like Stella and Becky. I try to locate an empty desk before they notice I have nowhere to sit.

'Did you have a buzz-y weekend, Bea?' Becky asks as she passes in a waft of sweet perfume. She catches Stella's eye and giggles.

'Yes, thanks,' I say, spying an empty seat by the window.

'Did you know,' Becky adds, 'that after a bee stings you it just drops down dead?'

'That's why they don't waste their stings on annoying stuff,' I say.

People are starting to look at me. This must be what happens when you lose 'buddy' status. Becky isn't smiling any more. 'Did you just call me annoying?'

'No, I was talking about bees.' A few people laugh. Becky gives me a death stare and thuds her bag down on the floor next to her desk.

'Oh, just leave her,' says Stella. 'She's not worth it.'

My stomach does a little flip. Something tells me Becky isn't a 'let's put this behind us' sort of person.

At lunchtime I sit by myself. In movies this would be when the shy kid comes over and sits with me and then we become best friends and nothing else matters after that.

No one comes over. As I eat, I feel a knot in my stomach, waiting for Stella, Becky and Jessica to arrive. The knot annoys me. I eat quickly, telling myself that it's because I'm really hungry. By the time I've finished and put my tray away, they still haven't joined the lunch queue. I feel the knot loosen a little. I don't have any lessons with them this afternoon.

As the bell rings at the end of the day, I wish Mum was picking me up after all. I feel as if I've had enough of my own company for one day.

When I get home, Dad opens the door.

'I thought you were supposed to be at work?'

'Hello, Dad, how lovely to see you,' he says, giving me a hug.

'I mean, why are you back so early?'

'Marginally better,' he smiles. 'I have to go away for a few days.'

I groan. 'How many is a few?'

'Only two or three. They need my initial survey faster than I thought. I'm going to run as many tests as I can in the field, rather than driving back and forth. I thought I'd go tonight, and then I'll be back before the weekend.'

Hester pads over, tail in the air. 'So we might be able to go flying at the weekend?'

'If the weather's good. Or we could try one of the hikes up in the hills.'

Not a total disaster. I stroke Hester as she rubs against my legs. 'Do we have any maps?'

'Good point. I'll check which ones we need.'

One of Dad's ideas for AW1—'After Work, Year 1'— is to set up an outdoor adventure company. When he was training to become a geologist, he had to look at lots of cliffs. So he decided he might as well learn how to climb them too. Being a geologist helps, because he knows which types of rock are dangerous to climb, and where to find safe ones. I've climbed a little bit, but Mum says it's not safe to learn the basics on an actual mountain, and we never stay anywhere long enough for me to join a proper club. In AW1, though, I will.

After dinner I open my laptop and search for hiking routes nearby. It turns out we are surrounded by forests and peaks. I glance at the homework piled at the end of my bed next to Hester. She looks at me hopefully.

'Ear tickling only after you've done my history homework,' I say. 'One of us needs to do it.' She rests her chin on her paws and closes her eyes. Maybe she's already studied World War 1.

I don't know how late I stay up researching, but the next morning I find it really hard to get out of bed. I walk-run to school and arrive just as the bell rings for first period.

I decide to start using my poky locker. Then at least I won't have a heavy rucksack to carry too. The only problem is that I still haven't learnt my lesson timetable. So, on Wednesday after break, I'm half-way to geography when I realize it's actually double chemistry and I don't have my enormous textbook.

I rush back through emptying corridors and fumble my locker open. As I reach for my book, I touch something sticky. I peer inside. The locker is smeared with a shiny substance which has a familiar smell. I lean in closer. Everything in my locker is covered in honey. I look down at the chemistry book in my lap. Both of which are now also covered in honey. I head to the toilets to clean myself up. I'm late for chemistry, but I don't tell the teacher why.

At lunchtime, Stella and her constellation sit nearby. When I walk past, they make a low buzzing noise, which ends in giggling.

A spark of anger glows in my chest. I remind myself what happens when bees sting. I try to push my frustration away, but there's nowhere for it to go. No one to share it with except Hester. Next period I have history with the full constellation. I head to the library to calm down. The constellation never comes here.

Miss James beckons me into the classroom. The only free table is behind Becky and tall-blonde-girl, who also goes by the name of Lauren. My history book is still covered in honey, so I walk up to the front to borrow the teacher's copy. Miss James is finishing a module of work which the rest of the class started weeks ago. I half listen, half plan what I will pack in my lunch for hiking and what extra kit I might need. I barely notice when she leaves the room to go and fetch something.

As soon as she has gone, Becky turns to Lauren and whispers, 'It's so rude to turn up to your lesson without your books.'

Lauren nods. 'Why do you think Bea had to change schools? Do you think she had to leave because no one liked her there, either?'

'There's not much to like,' agrees Becky. 'Maybe she did something really bad and they expelled her. That's normally why kids start halfway through the term.'

'Or maybe her parents did something really bad. Maybe they're on the run. Maybe her dad's some kind of criminal.'

Without thinking I reach out and grab a handful of Lauren's hair and pull. Her head jerks backwards and she cries out, but I don't let go. I pull harder. Lauren starts making a strange wailing noise.

Becky stands up. 'She's totally lost it,' she says, pointing at me but doing nothing to help Lauren. Just then, Miss James walks back into the classroom.

I feel my anger evaporate. Lauren is still wailing even though I've let go of her hair. The murmuring in the class gets louder.

'Quieten down,' says Miss James. 'Can someone please tell me what just happened?'

Becky puts her hand up. I know this isn't going to end well.

During final period, instead of maths I am leaning against the wall in a gloomy corridor. It smells faintly of disinfectant. There is the kind of eerie silence which only happens when people nearby are busy, behind closed doors. To my left is the Principal's office—I think. Everyone assumed I knew where I was going, but it didn't feature on Stella's familiarization tour.

After a few minutes, a distant voice calls, 'Come in.' The door must be very thick.

I step inside a bright office. A lady with neat hair and a green top stands up behind her desk.

'Beatrice, please come and sit down. Do you know why you're here?'

'I think so.' She looks at me expectantly. 'Is it because I pulled Lauren's hair in history?'

She raises her eyebrows. 'Until she cried. Partly. Mainly, Beatrice, it's because I don't think we've seen the best of you yet. I've been looking through your reports.' Here we go. I basically gave up trying at my last school. What was the point? We'd only move on again. 'It seems that you have a gift for languages. It seems that you have a gift for most subjects, but that at your previous school, your results fell off a cliff in the final term.' I wonder if she knows my dad is a geologist, or her joke was accidental. 'We don't tolerate poor behaviour at this school. But what I find equally unacceptable is not trying your best.' She searches my face for clues to how I'm taking this. I think I probably look upset. 'It's very important that we get off on the right foot here, and that we don't let bad habits take hold.' By 'we' of course she means 'me'. 'I haven't called your parents this time. But I want your assurance that I've made myself clear?' She smiles warmly at me. I find it impossible not to smile back. No one else has smiled at me yet today.

'Yes, Mrs Lewis.'

'Good. I don't want to see you in here again. Unless it's to share good news. Please close the door on your way out.'

'Yes, Mrs Lewis.'

I step back out into the corridor. I wonder if this marks the end or the beginning of my visits to Mrs Lewis's office.

*

When Dad comes home later, he doesn't give me a hug straight away, like he usually does. He takes his coat and shoes off before even realizing I'm there.

'Good trip?' I ask. I know he's only been gone three days, but it's felt like an eternity to me.

He rests his bag on the floor.

'I'm afraid I can't discuss it,' he says, in his serious Work Voice. I must look hurt because he adds, 'Sorry, darling, you know I can't talk about anything which might be sensitive for the company. Their share price could change overnight depending on what my reports say.'

'Yeah, I know. Top secret,' I say, trying to make light of it, but still feeling confused.

'How was today? Is school starting to feel a bit less new?' he asks.

'It was fine,' I lie. Fine is a good word for saying not very much.

'Good,' says Dad, 'I'm glad you're settling in.'

I'm not sure he's really listening. I'd hoped Dad would sense that something was wrong. That he'd try to make me feel better. I go to find Hester. She never cares about anything except Hester, but at least I know where I am with her. I never feel disappointed.

I lie on my bed and listen to Mum and Dad talking in low voices in the hall. I wonder if the top-secret rule applies to Mum, too.

At dinner time Dad is still in serious mode.

'I'm sorry, Bea,' he says in-between mouthfuls of pasta, 'I'm going to have to work this weekend.' I feel myself deflate. 'I've ordered a map and a hiking guide to some of the best routes round here. They might arrive tomorrow. You can look through and plan our first adventure.'

I don't mention that I've already discovered most of them.

'I'm sure we can find something to do together.' Mum turns to smile at me, the kettle in her hand. I really don't want to go shopping. 'Someone told me there's a bookshop in town.' She pauses, perhaps to allow this sensational news to sink in. 'It has kittens for adoption. They have free range of the shop. You can browse for books, or for a kitten. Oh, it also has a café.'

I stare at Mum's back while she makes tea.

'That sounds cool,' I say. 'That sounds very cool.'

'Good,' says Mum.

'Is this the same café you mentioned the other day?'

'Yes. You didn't seem very keen, but I thought I'd try again.'

'You didn't say there would be kittens,' I answer, feeling guilty that I just assumed all Mum wanted to do was shop. 'Don't tell Hester.'

Mum gives me an 'as if I would be that stupid' expression, which makes me giggle.

'If the kittens seem well cared for then perhaps we can think about adopting one.'

'Seriously?!' I rush over and give Mum a hug.

My gloomy feeling lifts a little, as I think about what kind of kitten Hester might find acceptable company. Probably one which lives in the garden and doesn't come inside. She would never actually make friends with another cat. I start to wonder if I'm a little bit like Hester.

Yutu 4

Sunrise casts a soft light around the wooden walls of my room. I love this time of day. Everything feels possible. I know Grandma's up, even though I can't hear her. She rises with the sun. I run through the packing list in my head. Spare clothes and mittens, torch, matches, flask, harpoon, hunting knife, rope. Some of the basic things I need will be in the cabin already. Grandma lets Petur use it as a stopover when he's hunting caribou.

I dress carefully, choosing my warmest top, and socks with no holes. I stuff my spare clothes into a watertight bag.

Grandma is sitting in an armchair sipping from a steaming cup of tea. Bannock bread sizzles gently in a pan. The doughy smell makes my stomach rumble.

'The bread should be ready. A small piece for me, and some *akutaq*, please,' Grandma says.

I lift the hot bannock bread onto a board and

slice it into chunks, giving myself twice as much as Grandma, with a large spoonful of the berry mix.

'Hungry today?' Grandma asks. 'You're growing again,' she smiles. A good appetite makes Grandma happy.

'I'm going to see Sami this morning, then we'll go to Tom's together later. I'll be back tomorrow, maybe in the evening, if that's OK.' I can't look at Grandma while I'm lying, so I stare at the bread instead, tearing it into chunks.

I can tell Grandma is watching me. My mouth feels dry and for a second I feel sure she knows I'm lying. If she asks me what I'm *really* doing, I will have to tell her.

'That sounds like fun. Tomorrow evening is fine.'

'Thank you,' I say. A wave of guilt washes away the fear. I don't feel guilty because I'm going to the cabin alone. I feel guilty because I'm lying.

I tidy up the breakfast things, then when Grandma heads off to the bathroom, I seize my chance. I take the bag from my bedroom, my harpoon and an extra chunk of bread.

'See you tomorrow, Grandma!' I call, then pull the front door shut behind me. I crunch round to the back of the house and pick up the plastic box of food. I stuff the bread on top, then walk as quickly as I can with a bag, box and harpoon towards Sami's house. There aren't many people around to see me. They're either at work, or not up yet. Sami's in the second category.

I dump my stuff in a heap on the ground outside the back of his house, then scoop up some snow. The first ball thuds right in the middle of Sami's window. Nothing happens. I make two more to throw, but Sami has pulled up the blind. He's clearly just woken up. His eyes are half open and his hair is at right angles. He pushes the window ajar. I stand underneath so that he can drop the key into my hands.

'Look after it,' he says sleepily. 'Spare fuel is on the back. See you tomorrow.'

'Thanks, Sami. I owe you,' I say.

'No worries,' he replies, pulling the window shut and drawing the blind down again.

I strap my stuff to the back of the snowmobile with a few bungees, then climb on and turn the key. Gently, I pull the starter cord and the engine growls into life. I glide away from Sami's house, towards the edge of town. I feel light, like powdery snow which lifts in the wind.

Sun sparkles across the lumpy sea ice in the bay. Dark patches of rock stain the tops of the hills which line the coast. I point the nose of the snowmobile towards the flat ground which lies between the hills and the sea ice. Cold wind rushes over my face. This is the route Petur has taken me on before. Just for day trips. This time, there is no one in front of me. No one to follow.

After about an hour, I slow to a stop, my hands tingling from the vibration of the engine. I take some bannock bread from the plastic box and lean my elbows on the saddle while I eat. Apart from the gentle creaking of the sea ice, and the swish of wind on the tundra, it is completely silent. Pale blue sky stretches across the horizon. There are no buildings in sight. No people. I try to imagine having a proper sledge with a team of dogs to pull it, like the one Grandma used when she was little. Grandma says the dogs were part of the family. It must have felt amazing to glide along without an engine buzzing in the background. Just the crunching of paws in the snow, and the hiss of the runners.

I rev the engine and slowly gather speed, heading inland for the last stretch. The cabin is in a hollow, tucked away from the stormiest weather.

A low hill comes into view. It has a wide natural overhang, like the crest of a rocky wave. It's not until I'm almost level with the overhang that the cabin appears. Although man-made, it blends into the landscape. The wood has weathered to a pale grey, and there is nothing shiny or sharply angled to make it stand out. The door is bolted shut to keep out any animals. There is no lock. The only people who pass this way, know who the cabin belongs to.

I slide the bolt and the door creaks open to reveal a neat, cosy space. A raised platform at the back is covered in caribou skins for sleeping. Various tools and equipment are stored in one corner. The other side is left clear for cooking and sitting. I sling my bag on the caribou skins and breathe in the earthy smell, somewhere between animal skins and smouldering fire.

I eat, sip some water, then pick up the harpoon and head outside.

It takes me half an hour to reach the shore on foot. It feels good to walk, like I'm really in the tundra, not just passing through.

Most people wouldn't know where the land stops and the sea ice begins, but I know. I can read the different patterns in the ice, the shapes and textures.

Using one arm to shield my eyes from the sinking sun, I move slowly and quietly, looking for signs of a seal's blowhole, or a lair. If the shapes look promising, I use my harpoon like a probe, testing the ice for a hollow spot or a hole.

After an hour, I am about a hundred metres from the shore. The sun glows orange in its final descent. It's time to head back to the cabin. I don't want to be on the sea ice after dark. It will be impossible to tell whether the patches of water are safe or not. There has been no sign of seals. Nothing. Not even the splashing sound as one slips beneath the ice before you spot it. No dark shapes squirming across the ice in the distance.

I feel frustrated. I didn't even have a chance to hunt.

As I crunch back through the snow, Grandma's words run through my head, about the seals and caribou disappearing. About how the things which made our people great, are disappearing one by one.

Perhaps she need never know that the bay was empty. My frustration is turning into a plan. There is another bay close by. It's just a little further north. Petur has told me about it. I will follow the shoreline round. If I leave at sunrise, I should have time to hunt and make it back home before dark.

No one will be disappointed.

Bea 4

My alarm goes off. I can't believe the weekend is over. Again. Dad barely emerged from his office. Before I get out of bed, I hear the front door gently closing. He's left for work already. I guess I'll have to tell him about the kitten-bookshop-café some other time.

It's OK, because I have a plan. I'm going to work hard too. There are only so many hiking routes I can plan. I need to focus on something else before Mum signs me up for ballet or cross-stitch somewhere.

Everyone seems to have forgotten about me over the weekend. Even Stella and the constellation seem to have lost interest. Or so I thought. No one mentions the honey or my visit to the Principal, but everyone knows. I catch whispered words and curious glances. Not just from Stella and the gang. I am becoming 'one to watch', and not in a good way.

I spend a lot of time in the library, or a bench in the corner of the playground where no one bothers to go because it's always in the shade. I barely speak to any other students until Wednesday morning. Then in chemistry we are assigned partners for the lab work. The teacher pairs me with a blond boy called Will. Will picks up his bag and walks over to join me. He doesn't look thrilled about being my partner, but he doesn't look upset either, which is good because we're going to be partners for the rest of term.

'Hey,' he says. 'Are you the new girl?'

'Newish. I'm Bea.'

'I'm Will.'

So far, so good. No buzzing noises or insect references. I'm not sure the conversation is going to develop much, though.

He stares at the instruction sheet we've been given for today's experiment. 'Do you know what we have to do?'

'Yeah. It's simple organic chemistry.'

Will looks at me, confused.

I start setting up the equipment, and he realizes I wasn't joking about the 'simple' part.

'Cool,' he says.

We finish first and the teacher is impressed. We also get correct results for each part of the experiment.

'Are you some kind of science genius?' Will asks, as we pack our things away.

'I just read the instructions,' I say, which is basically true.

As we walk out of class, Will heads off with some friends. Stella walks past with Lauren.

'Watching you flirt is disgusting,' Lauren hisses.

I wait until they've disappeared down the corridor, before walking to my next lesson.

At lunchtime the buzzing noises start again. This time Stella joins in with the others. They are sitting two tables away from me, so plenty of people can hear. They look around, smiling, wondering what the joke is. I finish my lunch as quickly as possible, then go to the library to start an English assignment.

I have chemistry again on Friday. I head to my locker, which I've finally had time to clean. Inside are all my textbooks, except the big red one I need for chemistry. I know I put it back on Wednesday. Someone has been in my locker again.

The bell rings so I head to class.

'Hey,' says Will, 'I thought you weren't coming.'

'I was looking for my textbook,' I say.

'You can share mine,' he says, pushing his chair closer. There is a waft of whatever he uses to make his hair stick up. It smells of bubblegum. It seems weird that he smells like a sweet.

We sail through our experiment again. When the teacher comes over to find out why we're doing nothing, Will shows her the write-up which he's already completed.

'Great teamwork,' she says. 'You've set the bar for everyone else.'

Will grins at me. I get the impression this is an improvement on his usual feedback for chemistry.

I look around the class to see who else has finished, and spot Stella staring at me with an expression of pure hatred. It seems that having someone to talk to twice a week comes at a price. An icy wave passes through my stomach, as an awful thought finally dawns on me.

Stella likes Will.

Yutu 5

For a split second I forget where I am. My face is cold, but I am warm beneath layers of heavy caribou skin. I push them to the side and reach for my boots which are at the other end of the bed. Everything on the raised sleeping platform stays warmer than on the floor. I slept in my clothes but slip my coat on straight away. I mustn't let my body heat escape. I eat the seal meat which I saved from the night before and have a sip of water, then pull on my mittens.

I push open the cabin door and gather up my bag, box and harpoon. Outside the air is fresh but freezing. I strap my things to the back of the snowmobile and brush a few flakes of snow from the seat before climbing on. To my right, the horizon glows pale orange below thin dark clouds. Straight ahead is a wide natural path between two small hills. I know the land around here, the shape of the bays beyond.

I've looked at maps, I've listened to Petur, but I've never actually been.

I pull the starter cord and the engine growls. I steer away from the cabin, northwards. As I leave the shelter of the rocky overhang, a fierce wind presses against me, blowing in from the sea. It's hard to keep a straight course, so I drive a bit faster. The snowmobile bumps and jerks over uneven ground.

After an hour or so, the sky is barely any lighter. The sun has risen above the horizon, now obscured by a band of cloud, spreading out across the frozen bay. I pass between the two small hills and head down towards the shore. Before I reach the sea ice, there is a patch of spruce, their branches crusted in snow. I slow down and steer the snowmobile through a narrow gap, into the cluster of trees. At least here my stuff will be sheltered from the wind until I'm ready to leave.

I estimate that I have two hours before I need to head back. I can't risk travelling in the dark. Anyway, Grandma will be waiting for me.

I slide my harpoon from underneath the bungee and walk down to the sea ice. The bank of grey cloud has crept closer. There's enough light to distinguish the types of ice and snow, but the wind is making it harder to see. It's stronger than when I left the cabin.

I follow the shoreline, heading north. I probe the ice before stepping onto patches of seawater. There is almost always solid ice beneath, but I don't want to take any chances.

Perhaps half a kilometre ahead, I see a dark shape on the ice. It might be a seal. I feel a surge of excitement. I head towards it, slowly. Seals have very bad eyesight, and the wind is in my favour. Even if it does spot me, there may be others nearby, and blowholes where they might surface. I picture myself dragging a seal back to Grandma's house. In this daydream I only have one seal, but one is enough.

A few flakes of snow begin to fall. I should turn back soon, but I've almost arrived at the sheet of ice where I saw the seal. It's wide and mostly flat, with a few bumps towards the centre. Placing each foot with care, I move towards the middle. I stop to probe the ice, checking for a possible lair. There is a long, high-pitched, creaking sound. The ground beneath my feet feels suddenly soft. I look down as seawater creeps up around the edges of my boots. I plunge down with the harpoon and there is nothing solid beneath, only freezing seawater. My heart starts to thump. I turn and take two quick strides in the direction of the shore. The ice doesn't give way, but I daren't stop. Perhaps this whole section of the bay is unstable.

I want to take the shortest route to the shore, but it's safer to retrace my steps. I know that route is solid. I try to work out which way I came, but the light is fading so fast I can't see my footprints. I feel myself begin to panic. I need to get off the sea ice now, but if I move too quickly, there's more chance I won't spot the weaker patches, or that my foot will press down too hard. I cannot go under. There is no one here to help me get back out.

I'm unable to retrace my steps. I have no choice. I will have to take the shorter route. The shore is only ten metres away.

The wind whips against my hood. I take a few more steps towards another ice sheet. I test the edge and it feels solid. I move slowly towards the centre then glance up. I'm five metres from the shore. Almost close enough to jump. I step again, and my foot disappears beneath the white crust. I throw myself forwards and sprawl onto my stomach as my right leg sinks into the freezing water. My left knee rests just above, on the edge of the ice which caved. Pain sears through the submerged leg, as water seeps beneath my layers of clothing. I use my arms to haul myself out in a commando crawl, but the water is weighing me down, pulling me under. The ice beneath my arms is sinking too. I push forwards again, my shoulders burning. I manage to get my right knee on top of the ice. It's numb with cold; I can barely move it, but I keep pushing until my whole body is on what's left of the ice sheet. Slowly, I drag my knees towards my chest and stagger to my feet.

I am gasping for breath but all I can hear is the wind, pressing against me, forcing me sideways. In front is a ridge of lumpy snow-covered ice. I slide my left foot forwards, then my right, and step over the ridge. My right leg is heavy with water. With the next step I reach the shore. My leg gives way and I stumble to the ground.

Snow whips through the air. I look across the sea ice trying to locate the cluster of spruce trees sheltering the snowmobile. Grey-white snow clouds merge with the grey-white land. I can barely see more than ten metres. The trees must be a kilometre away. I'm no longer even certain in which direction I should be looking. With a bolt of panic, I realize that I am disorientated. My clothes are wet. Soon, the damp will seep through from the outer layers and then my whole body will start to feel as cold and numb as my leg. I must keep moving.

The ground along the shore edge is mostly snow-covered boulders. They are exhausting to walk over and it's easy to slip and break an ankle. I decide to head further inland. From there I will find a flat path back to the spruce trees.

Using my harpoon for support, I climb the ridge separating the shore from the grasslands. It's only a few metres high, but my leg aches with cold. The wind is almost strong enough to blow me over. It whistles around me, pulling at my clothes.

I find it hard to think clearly. I must get back to the snowmobile. My food is there, and some dry clothes. I need to take my wet layers off as soon as possible. There's no way I will make it back home before dark now. Maybe I can stay in the cabin tonight and leave first thing in the morning. I think about Grandma waiting for me at home. I think about her speaking to Tom's parents and finding out that I wasn't there last night. That I'd lied. Sami was right. This trip wasn't the way to make Grandma worry less. I'm going to make her feel worse. Much worse.

As I reach the top of the ridge, a gust of wind knocks me off my feet and I roll halfway down the other side. When I stop, I am lying face down. Snow powder has forced its way under my hood. I brush some more from my face. I realize that I am shivering. My body has started to cool down much faster than I thought. I reach for my harpoon and push myself up. Snow-covered boulders lie to my left, so I keep moving forwards. I must not stop, whatever happens. That is how you freeze to death. Maybe ten minutes later, the ground starts to flatten out, and it's easier to walk.

I look up for some clue to which direction I should take. I decide to keep the wind behind me. It was blowing onto the shore when I left the snowmobile, so that should lead me back to where I began. I start walking again. It seems harder work than before. Perhaps I am feeling weaker. I've had nothing to eat for a few hours. There is some bread tucked inside my jacket but I daren't take my mittens off. I can't afford to let any more body heat escape.

Because I am surrounded by white, it's almost impossible to know how far I've come, or how long I've been walking. There is no sign of the spruce trees. I've stopped shivering, but I'm starting to feel sleepy. I wonder if I should have a rest. My coat would make a good place to lie down. Instead I keep putting one foot in front of the other. After a few more minutes I come to a stop. I don't know why. Perhaps it's because my right foot is numb. My left foot is very cold now too. I'm tired of walking against the wind. Something deep inside my brain tells me that I have hypothermia, that this is how you feel when your body gets so cold you can't think straight any more. I try not to think about what happens next to people who get this cold.

Just as I am about to have a rest in the snow, I see a dark shape within the swirling blizzard. I stumble towards it. It looks like a small hut. Some of the wooden boards have fallen off. I find a door and push the handle. The door creaks open. My head starts to spin. I can't make it stop, so finally I do what I was planning to do anyway. I lie down on the floor and close my eyes.

Bea 5

I pad down the stairs like Hester and knock quietly on Dad's office door. Silence.

'Dad, it's me.' I hear a rustle of papers.

'Yes, darling, come in.'

Dad looks up from his work. He has dark circles under his eyes. He looks tired.

I sit on the chair in the corner. 'Are you going to be working all weekend again, or just today?'

'I'm sorry, darling, a big thing has come up. It might be all weekend again.'

I chew my lip a little. 'How about next week-end?'

'Next weekend, I hope, will be better.'

He smiles at me, but it doesn't reach his eyes. They seem alive with a different energy. Almost like he is anxious about something. Uneasy.

I potter back to the kitchen. Mum is busy doing something with flour.

'I unpacked the last box of shoes and boots yesterday. I think your hiking trainers are too small for you. Shall we go into town today to get some new ones? We can see what other hiking equipment they have in there. You probably need some leggings too, or a fleece.'

'OK,' I nod suspiciously. 'But no clothes shops?'

'All right, all right. Hiking paraphernalia only.'

We head into town after breakfast. It seems as if every other shop sells some sort of outdoor equipment. Mum suggests we try one of the larger stores because there will be more choice.

I walk past the section with rucksacks and tents, to clothes and shoes, and start looking at fleeces.

'The best warm, lightweight material is silk,' Mum says. I look at her, trying to hide my surprise. 'There are lots of high-performance man-made fabrics, but silk is still the best base layer.'

She wanders over to look at boots. I stare at the fleeces for a little longer, wondering why Mum knows so much about kit. Perhaps the Venn diagram for shopping and more exciting pastimes overlaps in outdoor clothing shops.

After an hour of choosing and trying, I have boots, a fleece and some brilliant leggings with skulls. I'm ready to leave, but Mum suggests going for a drink somewhere. I'm lining up my reasons for going home when I remember the kitten-bookshop-café. I can tell that Mum is pleased when I seem keen.

We gather up the bags and head kitten-wards.

Mum orders two hot chocolates with whipped cream. Her first sip deposits a giant whipped-cream moustache beneath her nose. I expect her to wipe it away, and then head to the loo in search of a mirror. Instead she pretends not to have noticed, even when two customers sit down at the adjacent table. I start to giggle. We try to decide which is better, a beard or a moustache. I say beards are better because they keep you warm, but Mum thinks moustaches win because you can change the shape to match what you're wearing. Typical.

I realize that most of the time I spend with Mum is at home, or with Dad around. We hardly ever go anywhere together. She doesn't mention manicures once.

Dad spends most of Saturday in his office. On Sunday he actually goes in to work.

By dinner time on Sunday evening, days have passed since we've talked to each other. Lots has happened, but when we're sitting down to eat, I'm not sure what to say. He doesn't even pretend to smile.

I don't think my news is the right kind to cheer him up. Then just before we clear the table, his phone buzzes. Instead of ignoring it, he pushes back his chair, and leaves the room, staring at the screen as he walks.

Ambush

I like my new routine of schoolwork and library. It isn't exactly fun, but it's mostly buzz-free.

As Wednesday approaches I feel the knot in my stomach begin to grow. I see Will around school, but never with Stella. I don't know if they're together. There's no one I can ask. I hope they aren't, for Will's sake.

On Wednesday morning I head to my locker before remembering that there's no point. My chemistry book hasn't reappeared.

As I take my seat next to Will, I feel Stella's eyes on me. On us.

'Did you find your book?' Will asks.

'Not yet. Do you mind if we share again?'

'Sure.' He seems pleased. 'Where is your accent from? I was trying to figure it out.'

Before I have a chance to answer, the teacher starts talking. Today we're doing something complicated with electrodes. Will helps me to set everything up. The teacher walks around and nods approvingly.

'Can anyone tell me how we know if the gas we've collected is hydrogen?' she asks.

I put my hand up. 'It makes a squeaky popping noise,' I say.

'Well done, Bea, yes.'

Will smiles at me and raises his eyebrows. 'Excellent answer, Einstein.'

I decide not to tell him that Einstein was a physicist.

After the lesson, Will walks with me towards the cafeteria. I can't think of an excuse to walk on my own. Even though I would prefer to.

'Which part of town are you in?' he asks.

'Over by the airport. My dad uses one of the planes there.'

'What, like flies it himself?'

'Yes, for work.'

'Have you ever been in it with him?'

'He takes me with him when he can.'

'That's so cool,' Will says. 'How many seats does it have?'

'Four.' He looks hopeful.

'You're so lucky,' he says. One of his friends waves from the back of the lunch queue. 'Gotta go. See you later.'

After he's gone, I feel strange. Relieved, but also exposed. Apart from when I was Stella's buddy, no one has really walked anywhere with me between lessons. While Will was there, no one made any nasty comments, or buzzing noises. Or if they did, I didn't notice.

In form time, the buzzing is now mixed in with squeaky popping sounds. So inventive. It's mostly Becky and Lauren, but other people seem to be joining in if they feel like it.

When the bell rings, I grab my bag, and head to the toilets. As I push the door, I am aware that someone is right behind me. Before I can turn round, they shove me towards one of the cubicles. My shoulder hits the door which slams open against the cubicle wall. Whoever is behind me forces me to my knees. I feel a hand on the back of my head, pressing it towards the edge of the toilet seat. When my chin is almost touching it, a voice whispers, 'You shouldn't steal other people's boyfriends.' It sounds like Lauren.

'It's not nice,' hisses another voice I don't recognize. 'If you don't stop, then next time your head will go inside the toilet.'

'And we'll give you a wash,' says the one who sounds like Lauren.

The hand lifts from my head. I hear feet running to the toilet door.

I get up and lock the cubicle. I put the toilet lid down and sit for a few minutes. I feel cold. Seconds before I was sweating. My heart is pounding. I didn't have a chance to react, now the adrenaline is making me feel weak and shaky. I feel ashamed that I allowed someone to do this to me.

They were clever enough not to name names or let me see their faces. I guess that clears things up about Will and Stella.

I unlock the door and walk over to the sinks. I stare at myself in the mirror. The face which stares back looks paler than I'd hoped, and frightened. I wash my hands and brush my hair away from my face. I realize that my hand is shaking. The spark of anger reignites in my chest. How dare they push me onto the floor. How dare they threaten me. Stella could have talked to me instead. If she had, I would have told her that I'm not interested in her boyfriend. It doesn't matter if she is a coward though. I can still do the maths. There's one of me, and lots of them.

I take a deep breath and walk to my next lesson.

*

When I get home from school, I go straight to my room and sit on my bed. I need some space to think about what happened today.

'Beatrice, is that you?' Mum shouts.

'Hi, Mum, just getting my homework out of the way.'

Hester nudges the door open and pads over. When I don't stroke her, she stares up at me with her big amber eyes.

'Are you really the only living, breathing thing that is interested in how I feel, Hester?' She sits neatly, with her tail curled round her paws. Her gaze drifts to the window and the birds outside.

I know Hester has more important things to focus on.

I play today's events back in my head, over and over. I imagine Lauren and the other girl, laughing about how easy it was, how I did nothing to defend myself. *It's not nice. We'll give you a wash.* Their words echo round and round.

'Bea, dinner time!' Mum calls.

I'm lying on my bed next to my unopened school bag. I must have fallen asleep.

I walk slowly downstairs, just as Dad comes in through the front door.

'Hi, darling,' he says, and gives me a tight smile. He takes off his coat and shoes with a sort of robotic urgency. 'With you in a moment,' he adds when he sees me watching.

'Still cold outside,' Dad says as he sits down for dinner. He looks at the pot on the table. 'Smells good.'

Dad is chatty, but it's a weird chatty. Sort of forced. I'm glad though, I don't feel like talking at all.

'Bea, do you have any after-school plans tomorrow or Friday?' he asks.

'Err, no,' I say, 'definitely no plans.'

'OK,' says Dad. 'Only—make sure you come straight home, won't you.'

'After school?'

'Yes.'

'Why, is something happening?'

'No.' He pauses. Maybe he's realized how weird he's sounding. After a few seconds he adds, 'I might be home early, that's all, and it would be nice to see more of you.'

My mum is looking at Dad with an expression which hovers somewhere between confusion and concern.

'Well, it would be lovely if you are able to come back a bit earlier,' she says.

*

The next evening, Dad is back super late. Before he comes home, though, he phones Mum to make sure I'm here.

She doesn't mention it to me, but I hear the phone ring, and Mum saying, 'Yes, she's upstairs in her room. We're both fine.'

So much for being back early.

On Friday, I make my way to chemistry before the bell even rings.

I sit down quietly next to Will.

'Hey,' he says. 'I think we're just doing theory today. No experiment.'

A wave of relief washes over me.

I never imagined that chemistry theory could make me feel that way.

We write for most of the lesson. At one point I accidentally catch Stella's eye. She stares at me defiantly, with no hint of shame.

When the bell rings, I make sure that I am first out of the door. I spend lunchtime in the library, then head to my final period. I watch the minute hand move slowly round the clock. When the bell rings this time, I wait for everyone else to go. Stella and her gang are always in a hurry to get home on Friday. I should be able to leave in peace.

First I need to collect my textbooks. I haven't been

to my locker for two days. I couldn't face any more nasty surprises. I take a deep breath and unlock the door. I look inside before putting my hand in. There is something resting on top of the books. I take it out and stare at it. It's a jar of honey. It's small but looks expensive. There's a piece of honeycomb floating in the middle. Around the neck of the jar is an elastic band with a small square of paper attached. On the square of paper, someone has drawn a little smiley face in gold pen. I'm fairly sure it's a gift.

Maybe I should feel grateful that someone has left me a gift. Instead I feel annoyed. I don't need people to feel sorry for me. I just wish everyone would leave me alone.

Surprise

I expect Dad to be working all weekend again, but he comes home on time. I still get the tight-smile treatment, then after he's changed out of his work clothes, he knocks on my bedroom door and asks me to come downstairs.

I appear in the kitchen to see Mum wearing a look of anticipation which probably mirrors my own.

Dad follows me in, and walks towards the kettle, then seems to change his mind and ends up standing at one end of the table, as if he's about to address a roomful of people.

'I have to go away with work for a few days,' he begins. He's looking at Mum, but it feels like he's talking to both of us.

Is this why he called me downstairs? Hardly news-flash material. I glance over at Mum, who is looking at Dad with an encouraging sort of smile. She clearly thinks he's lost it too.

'I'll be travelling about as far north as you can sensibly go. It's just within range for the four-seater. I need to fly up on Saturday, then fly back Sunday afternoon, possibly Monday.' I think I've adopted the encouraging smile now too. 'I just thought,' he adds matter-of-factly, still looking at Mum, 'that it might be OK for Bea to miss one day of school and come with me. I think it could count as education. She'll get to see parts of the country which aren't really accessible by land.' He turns to look at me now. 'I know I've been too busy to hike for the last few weekends. Maybe this will make up for it. A little bit.'

The kitchen is so silent, I can hear myself breathing. I look over at Mum. She frowns and says, 'Do you think it's safe to go all that way in a tiny plane?'

She hasn't said no. There's still hope. But only if I manage to keep my mouth shut.

'These planes are some of the safest in the world,' Dad says. 'They function better in cooler temperatures, like most planes, and they have one of the best accident records. We'll be safer than travelling somewhere in our car.'

'Where will you stay?' Mum asks.

'There's a small settlement nearby. Work has arranged for someone to collect me. I just need to call when we get there.'

Mum looks at me, 'Do you want to go, Bea? Is there anything important on at school, this Monday?'

I must not sound too keen.

'I'd really like to see some more of the wilderness. It would be so cool to say I'd been to the Arctic Circle. I mean, if I take photos then perhaps I can use them for a geography module or something.'

'Hmmm,' Mum says. 'Can you leave me and Dad alone to talk about this?'

'OK,' I say, trying to sound stoic.

Inside my heart is singing. Mum only has a chat *alone* with Dad when she needs to iron out the terms. She's going to let me go.

I am going away for the weekend!

Flight

I sit on the bottom step of the stairs. My T-shirt is sticking to my back. I wish Dad hadn't told me to wear my thermal layers. I know it's going to be cold where we're going, and it's not very easy to get changed in a four-seater aeroplane, but it's hot on our stairs. I take my coat off.

Excitement fizzes in my stomach. I want to leave before Mum decides this is a bad idea and Dad should go without me. A hundred cat cafés couldn't offset that disappointment.

'Dad! I'm ready,' I shout in the direction of his office.

After a minute or so Dad emerges, pale-faced. 'Where's Hester?' he asks. Dad has never shown any interest in my cat.

'She's on my bed. Don't forget to say goodbye to Mum, too,' I add quietly. Perhaps a few days away will be good for Dad as well as for me. I know it's a work trip, really, but even he can't be glued to his laptop and fly a plane at the same time.

Dad comes back downstairs with Mum. He heads to the door, picking up his bag on the way. I hadn't noticed it sitting packed and ready beneath the coats.

Mum gives me a hug. 'Enjoy your adventure,' she says. That's all. No list of potential dangers to avoid. As I gather my things, she adds, 'Look after Dad.' The tone of her voice makes me look up. She is waiting for an answer.

'Of course,' I say, trying to sound more casual than I feel. 'Dad doesn't need me to look after him.'

As I get into the car, Dad turns on the radio. He never listens to the radio. He tries a few different stations until he finds one playing music. He winces as the thumping baseline kicks in.

'Do you mind if I flick through?' I ask.

'Go ahead,' he says, sounding distracted.

We drive the rest of the way listening to something good. Normally I would be delighted. Today, I wish Dad and I were chatting about wind speed and journey times, like we usually do before a flight.

We breeze through the terminal. In fact, I have trouble keeping up with Dad. He almost seems to have forgotten I'm here.

There is no one to escort us to our plane this time.

I run-walk across the tarmac, my large bag thumping against my leg. We stow our things in the tiny baggage compartment and climb into the cockpit.

Dad clips in and starts checking the instruments. He seems to relax a little.

'Can you double-check the wind speed?'

'One-two-eight-delta-foxtrot, you are cleared for take-off, no delays,' crackles a voice through the radio.

We taxi down the runway then gather speed. The G-force pushes me into my seat as the plane lifts then climbs, the engine whining as we ascend.

After a few minutes we enter some light cloud. The plane rolls and bumps through the uneven pressure, then we break into clear sky.

'How high?' Dad asks.

'4,500 feet,' I say.

'Good. We'll stay at this altitude for most of the flight.'

He stares ahead and his expression begins to harden. I don't want serious Dad to return.

'So what's our ETA, Group Captain?' I can't believe I've actually said this.

Dad takes a second to reply. 'Flight time is around four hours. We should arrive well ahead of sunset.'

'OK.' I feel a flutter in my stomach, as I try to imagine landing in the Arctic.

'What will I do while you're working?'

'The company has a local contact who'll come to collect us.' Dad pauses. For a second he seems lost in thought again. 'I haven't told them that you're coming, but I'm sure it won't be a problem. Tomorrow you can have a look around. We'll be in one of the northernmost settlements. I think it's pretty small, but there'll be snow of course.'

I smile. 'How will we know when we've crossed into the Arctic Circle?'

'Well, it depends. Some people say it's where the treeline ends, so where it's too cold for anything big to grow; others say it depends on the average temperature, or you could just follow our map coordinates. Most maps have a circle drawn on them, to show the area where the sun doesn't rise for a whole twenty-four hours in mid-winter.'

I love the idea of being on top of the world, literally.

'So we won't be near any big towns?'

'We'll be hundreds of miles from almost everyone else in the world. Humans have messed around with nearly every part of the planet, except the Arctic.'

'So why are you going there for work?'

Dad stares straight ahead, his lips pressed tightly together.

'Nothing exciting. Just additional survey material.'

'But—'

'Perhaps it's time for a snack,' he says. 'Why don't you see what's in there?' He points vaguely behind the seats, without turning round.

I reach behind for a small sandwich bag, feeling confused. Dad wanted me to come, but I can't help thinking he'd rather I wasn't here.

'We still have a way to go. Did you bring anything to do?' he asks. 'I'm sorry, I didn't remind you.'

'Yeah, I have some music and a book,' I say, passing him an apple. He puts it down without taking a bite.

I finish mine in silence, then put my earphones in and rest my head against the window. Clouds merge to form a colossal bumpy duvet beneath us, obscuring my view of the ground. Thinner, wispier clouds spin out above. It's not quite the fun trip I'd imagined, but with every passing second, I am travelling further away from new house, new school, new streets. I close my eyes.

A sudden jolt startles me. I don't know how long I've been asleep. The plane shudders again.

I turn my head and see Dad gripping the side stick.

'It's OK,' he says, 'but I'm afraid we've hit some bumpy weather. There were medium winds forecast for the final part of our journey, but I'm afraid this is more like a Force Nine.'

A cold wave passes down my back.

'How far is the airport?'

'We're just beginning our descent.'

'What should I do?'

'Keep an eye on the altimeter and airspeed and be ready to take the controls if there's any kind of emergency.'

I swallow. 'OK.'

Dad turns to look at me. He smiles. In an instant it's gone, but it felt warm and reassuring, almost like a normal Dad smile.

We're surrounded by white. The clouds above and below have joined forces and we're inside a giant foggy mist, travelling at 170 knots.

'How can we land if we can't see where we're going?' I say.

'That's why we have all these instruments,' Dad says calmly. 'You don't actually need to be able to see, it's just a lot easier.'

'And safer?' I ask.

'If I'm not happy with our approach, I'll pull up and we'll try again. I programmed in the whole journey. The plane knows where it's supposed to go.'

The plane shudders and shakes in response. We

drop a few feet and my stomach lurches. I clutch the edges of my leather seat. My palms are sweaty.

As we descend, the engine makes a whiny noise.

'What's our altitude?' Dad asks.

'1,000 feet.' I don't think Dad needs me to check. He's keeping me busy.

The cloud seems thicker. It whips past the cockpit in smoky trails. As we reach 500 feet the plane develops a steady rattling sound.

Dad continues with the landing routine.

A dark shape appears within the swirling white. Without warning we emerge from the thickest cloud into a light mist. I can just make out the solid lines of a runway ahead. The dark shape is a building at the opposite end.

'Flaps down,' Dad says.

The ground approaches fast. I feel the wind pushing us to the left as Dad tries to hold us steady. The back tyres bump down, then the front, and the engine roars as Dad begins to brake. The propellers slow and we come to a gentle stop.

'That wasn't so bad after all,' Dad says. He turns to look at me. 'Well done, Wing Commander. I'm going to recommend you for promotion.'

'That was bumpier than I thought it would be,' I say, trying to sound calm.

'A bit different to the forecast,' Dad says. 'But it's already starting to lift a little.'

I look up and see that the mist is thinning out.

'Welcome to the Arctic,' Dad says. 'Why don't you stay here while I find out if my contact has arrived to show us where we'll be spending the night. No point in us both freezing.'

Dad trudges through the snow towards the small building. It makes me realize that airports don't need much to function. This one doesn't even have an air traffic control tower. There is only one other plane, a four-seater, similar to ours.

While I wait for Dad, I think about what the settlement will be like, and how people keep their houses warm when it's so cold outside. I'm glad Dad insisted on thermals now, and endless layers. I pause my daydream when I realize that he's been gone for a while. Maybe ten minutes. I unclip and put my coat on, zipping it right up to the top.

As I push open the door, icy air rushes in. I pull my hood up and step onto the snow. It's packed down hard, but not slippery.

I follow Dad's footsteps towards the building, my snow boots crunching on the frozen ground.

When I'm about ten metres away, I stop in my tracks. There's another sound. I strain to hear it above the wind. It's voices. Raised voices, coming from the building. I start walking again, slowly. One voice sounds like Dad's, then I hear someone shouting. There is a thump from inside the building, like something hitting the wall. I gasp, and run the last few metres, crouching down below the only window, my heart thudding.

I hear a man's voice again. Not Dad's. I can't make out what he's saying, he isn't shouting but he sounds angry. Dad starts to talk. It's easier to tune in to his words. I hear something about *lying*. The man says *no*, then Dad replies. The man shouts. There is another thump. I can't bear not seeing. I stand up and peer through the glass.

I can't work out what's going on. There are three people inside. One man is gripping Dad. Dad is wrestling to get free, then I see him slump to the ground.

For some reason I cannot move. My legs feel heavy. I look at Dad, lying motionless on the floor. It feels like minutes have passed, but it must be a split second. The man who was holding Dad is huge. He looks over to the window. Our eyes lock, his widen in surprise.

'I think we have another problem,' I hear him say slowly.

The other man follows his gaze, and his eyes rest on me.

'What are you waiting for?' says the smaller man. 'Get her. We don't know what she heard.'

The big man moves towards the door. Suddenly my feet unglue themselves.

I turn and run.

The door scrapes open behind me. I look left and right, my chest burning as I suck in the freezing air. There's nothing but white on either side. Nothing but snow. The only shape to interrupt the emptiness ahead, is our plane.

'We just want to talk to you!' the big man shouts.

I don't believe him.

'Who are you?' he shouts.

He swears, then I hear the *crunch-crunch* of running feet. He is coming after me. I must not turn round, it will slow me down. I'm only ten metres from the plane now. I sprint towards the passenger door, then at the last minute swerve towards the pilot's side. I fumble with the handle and swing the door open.

Through the cockpit window I can see the big man powering across the runway. I start the engine. I have no plan except to get away from him. The plane roars into life. The propellers start to spin. I drive forwards. The man waits until I'm level with him, then jogs alongside the passenger door. He grabs the handle and rattles it. As the plane gathers speed, he's forced to jump aside, but I'm running out of runway. Ahead is the building and the other plane. I need to turn around, which means slowing down. I steer hard to the right.

The big man loops to one side, avoiding the propellers, then he sprints towards my door. The smaller man has joined him. He shouts something, and they both stop running.

For a moment I am relieved, then I begin to understand. They don't need to chase me. There is nowhere for me to go. Eventually the plane will run out of fuel as I taxi up and down, and I will have to stop. Then Dad and I will both be in that little room with no one to help us.

The building is behind me again. The engine idling as I inch forwards. I press my face against the window and see both men standing at the side of the runway, waiting for me to give up. The door to the building swings open and Dad staggers out, clutching his head. He is looking at the plane. He shouts something towards me. I can just make it out above the drumming of the engine.

'Go!' he's shouting. 'Take off!'

The smaller man runs over to Dad. The bigger man starts walking in my direction. Perhaps he's decided not to take any chances.

I realize, with horror, that Dad wouldn't tell me to go if there were other options.

He thinks I can do it. The clouds have lifted. The visibility has improved. I line the plane up in the middle of the runway, my heart thumping, and begin to accelerate. I imagine Dad is sitting next to me, running through the flight checklist. I begin to feel strangely calm. When I concentrate on what I need to do, there is no space for panic.

The speedometer dial reaches seventy knots. There is a familiar heavy feeling as the plane lifts. The wheels leave the ground. I watch the altimeter tick past one hundred feet.

I am flying a plane. Solo. I push that thought from my head and focus on procedures.

I check airspeed, pitch and altitude. Visibility is OK beneath the clouds. I won't be able to rely on the altimeter because the air pressure may have risen since the storm passed. I need to stay low but cannot stay too low in case there is a hill or a tall building. The plane purrs through the air.

I look at the fuel gauge and my heart skips a beat. The tank is almost empty.

I scan the ground beneath. I need somewhere flat, but the landscape is a patchwork of snow-covered hills. The endless white makes my eyes ache. An alarm sounds. The fuel gauge is flashing.

I look desperately from left to right. A horseshoe-shaped ridge rises up ahead. I can't risk climbing higher with an empty fuel tank. To my left I spot a dark shape in the snow, like a small building.

As I focus on it, my perspective sharpens. Within the endless white, I can see that close to the hut, the ground flattens out.

I steer the plane round towards it. I check the altimeter and airspeed. I'm going too fast. I pull back as the plane descends. It's wobbling from side to side. I try to steady it, but it's hard to concentrate on everything at once. I stop looking at the altimeter and concentrate on what I can see. I'm still going too fast. A few metres above the snow, I pull up again. The back wheels hit the ground hard. The plane jerks from side to side. I pull on the brakes and the plane starts to spin slowly sideways, towards the building. I hold onto the controls. There's nothing more I can do. The plane lurches to the right, and my head hits the window.

Lost

I open my eyes. My head hurts. At first I can't work out where I am, then I remember Dad in the building, the men chasing me. Flying the plane on my own. I don't know how long I've been unconscious. Maybe only a few minutes. It's still light.

I lift my head from the window and gently touch my forehead. There is a smooth lump near my right temple.

My seat is leaning to one side. The plane has come to a stop against a small ridge. It's resting on the right-hand wing, which means the wheels must have come off. I'm lucky the fuel tank was empty and nothing caught fire.

I stare out at the snowy landscape and try to think straight. Who were those men? What have they done with Dad? They weren't expecting to see me. Were they expecting to see Dad, or did he surprise them too?

I shiver. I realize it's not just because I'm frightening myself. I am cold. I have no idea where I am. I have no idea where the nearest settlement is. I saw nothing from the air. No roads, nothing. All I have is what's inside the plane. I try not to panic.

I look through the window at the hut. This feels like a pointless place to build anything. It doesn't look big enough to live in, but if you did build a hut in the middle of the Arctic, so far from everywhere, you must have a good reason. It might have something useful inside.

I try to ignore the fact that the sky is growing gloomier. Soon it will be dark.

I don't want to leave the plane and step into the icy wind, but I need to see what's in the hut.

I put my hood up, then open the door. The plane has tilted so much the snow is up to the level of the door. It was cold inside the plane. Outside, the freezing air stings my face.

I stand next to the hut for a minute, listening. The only sound I hear is the wind.

The door isn't bolted. I lift the latch and push. The hinges creak. There are no windows. I have to let my eyes adjust to the gloom. I begin to make out shapes. There is a pan hanging on the wall. On the floor is some kind of bed, or pile of animal furs.

I walk over for a closer look. I bend down, and then leap back in shock. Within the pile of furs, is a boy's face, framed by a fur hood. His skin is pale. He looks about the same age as me.

I stand still and wait for my heart to slow a little, then I creep back towards the boy. I kneel down next to the furs. His lips are bluish. I remember learning that you can find out if someone's breathing by holding a mirror above their mouth, to see if it steams up. I have no mirror, but I could check for a pulse. I don't want to move the furs to find his wrist. I know there are other places where your pulse can be strong, like your neck, or your temples. I reach over and place two fingers on his temple, level with his left eye.

I feel nothing, then just as I am about to remove my fingers, there is a gentle bump. I keep very still. There is another bump. He is alive.

Why is he here?

I look around the hut for clues. There are a few wet patches on the floor. Some of them are from the snow on my boots. The others were already there. I don't think he can have been in the hut very long.

I lift the edge of the rug to see what he is wearing. Perhaps that will give me some idea of where he's come from. It's surprisingly heavy. In the dim light, I can just make out that he is wearing ski trousers and some kind of thick jacket. He is also wearing snow boots. One of them has a puddle of water beneath it. I touch the edge of the ski trousers. They are soaking wet. I look at his face again. His lips are still a faint bluish colour. I think he might have hypothermia. Dad taught me about it. If you go for long hikes, it's something you need to look out for. Thinking about Dad makes tears prick my eyes. I try to focus on what I know. If you get really cold, then sometimes it's not possible to warm you up again. Not unless you're in hospital. There's no hospital near here. I'm the only chance he has.

I make a decision. I'm going to get my stuff. Perhaps it's a stupid idea. It might be warmer in the plane, but I really don't want to be on my own, and the boy needs my help. Night is falling, so I have to be fast.

I start piling luggage in the snow: my bag, Dad's bag, the emergency kit and a blanket. I go to the cockpit and tug the sandwich things out from behind the chair.

I run over to the hut with the biggest bag and sling it inside, then I come back for the rest.

I find my torch and hang it from the door handle,

then I sit on the floor and begin to play back everything that happened after landing the plane. Dad walking to the building. Seeing those men through the window, Dad collapsing on the floor. I get as far as accelerating down the runway when I realize my whole body is beginning to shake. I pause. It's too much to think about in one go. I also need to help the boy. With every passing second he must be getting colder.

I peel back the rugs, then tug gently at his right boot until it slides off. Water spills onto the floor. I pull off his sock and then the other boot, which is dry. If I'm going to warm him up, I know it's essential to remove any wet clothes. I pull at the ski trousers, peeling them down one leg at a time then reach for the blanket and wrap it around his legs and feet, draping the driest fur rug on top of that. I try to heave him into a more upright position. He begins to stir. This must be a good sign. He's not too deeply unconscious.

I look for the lunch bag in the pile of luggage. My stomach twists uncomfortably. I've had nothing to eat since the apple. It reminds me of the apple which Dad didn't touch. I start to wonder whether someone has found him, or if he's still with those men, and if they will give him something to eat.

I sit next to the boy and pour a tiny amount of hot

tea into the lid of Dad's flask, then hold it up to his lips. Slowly, I tip the cup. A small amount of tea runs down his chin. I lean his head back a little further and try again. I manage to get some in his mouth. I see the top of his neck move as he swallows, so I try the same amount again, then a little more. After one whole cup, the boy's eyes flicker open. At first he doesn't seem able to focus on anything, then he turns to look at me. His eyes are the darkest brown.

'I think you have hypothermia,' I say.

He looks down at the cup in my hand. I fill it again and lift it to his mouth. He drinks it all. He looks around the room, like he's trying to piece together the same mystery as me. Where did he come from? How did he get here?

Just when I think he's about to close his eyes again, he speaks. It makes me jump, even though his voice is quiet.

'Is it dark outside?' he asks, so softly that I can barely hear. He has an accent I cannot place.

'Yes, since about an hour ago,' I reply.

'Can I have some more tea?' he asks. I pour another cup.

It seems incredible that the lifeless person beneath the rugs is now talking to me. Asking for tea.

I'm so glad not to be alone. Only this morning

I couldn't wait to fly away and leave everyone behind.

I realize that I am starting to feel very cold too. I need to eat. I take a packet of sandwiches from the lunch bag. I wonder whether they were mine or Dad's. I have no appetite, so I try to imagine Dad is here, telling me to eat up. I know he would think it was silly to go hungry. My mouth is dry, so I pour myself a small amount of tea, to help the sandwich go down. The boy is watching.

'Would you like something to eat?' I ask.

'Yes,' he replies, but doesn't move. I wonder if he can.

'Are you hurt?' I ask.

He shakes his head. 'I'm not hurt. I am just feeling weak.'

I nod. I position the sandwich so that he can take a bite.

He chews very slowly. His face is still pale, but his lips aren't blue any more. After a few minutes have passed, he speaks again.

'I think you might have saved my life.'

I wonder whether anyone has come to Dad's rescue. Whether someone has saved his life. Or spared it.

A minute or so passes before the boy adds, 'Why are you here?'

He is looking at me like I'm some kind of unicorn. A girl, alone, in the middle of a frozen wilderness. Yet a few hours ago, I discovered him, alone, in the same wilderness, soaking wet, even though I saw no lakes or water when I was coming into land.

'I—' Nothing else comes out. I try again. 'I lost my way,' is all I manage to say. Biggest understatement ever.

Part of me wonders whether any of this is happening at all, or if I step outside the hut again, I'll be back at the airport and Dad will be returning from the building at the end of the runway, smiling.

'I fell through the sea ice,' he says.

'You *fell* through some ice?' I say.

'Sea ice,' he corrects. 'I was hunting for seals. I shouldn't have gone alone. I fell through the ice. Many people die that way.' His voice is clearer now. Stronger.

I begin to understand what he's telling me.

'The sea is near here?'

'You really don't know where you are, do you?'

'I must have missed a signpost,' I say defensively.

He tilts his head to one side and looks confused. He wasn't trying to make me feel stupid. He's just surprised.

I realize how tired I am. Instead of words, all that comes out is a sob, a noise which doesn't even really sound like it's come from me.

I am aware of the boy trying to move, rubbing his legs and his arms.

'What happened?' he says. 'Can you tell me?'

Something about the boy's voice makes me feel calmer.

I think about how unreal my story will sound. How unbelievable. Then I remember the aeroplane outside the hut.

The boy is staring at me, waiting.

I take a deep breath.

'I flew up here, with my dad. He has a plane.'

The boy doesn't nod or say anything. He is letting me take my time.

'Dad was coming for work. We were supposed to meet someone at the airport. When we got there, two men were waiting for my dad.'

I stop talking as the tears roll down my face.

Still, the boy waits.

'They attacked him. Then they came after me. I ran away, back to the plane.' I pause. 'I managed to take off, and—'

'You *flew* a plane?' The boy's expression has remained completely unchanged. Now his mouth hangs slightly open, and the hint of a smile spreads up to his eyes.

'Yes, I flew it here. But I ran out of fuel. The landing was bad, and I nearly crashed into this hut. I didn't know you were inside.'

The fact that I nearly crashed an aeroplane into the hut where he was sheltering doesn't seem to bother him. He's more interested in the fact that it happened at all.

'How did you learn? Who taught you to fly a plane?'

'My dad,' I sniff.

'Have you done it before? Flown on your own, I mean.'

'No. I don't think it's even legal.'

He slumps back against the wall, but his eyes are shining. Definitely much better than when I arrived.

I don't want to talk any more, but he keeps on asking questions.

'Do you know who the men were? The ones who attacked you.' It's almost as if he's been reading my mind.

'I have no idea.' I shake my head slowly. 'There was one other plane at the airport. I thought it must be theirs.'

'They have a plane too?' the boy says.

'Yes, a four-seater like the one I was flying.'

The boy stares at the wall, like he's thinking something over. After a few minutes he says, 'They might come looking for you.'

A coldness runs through me. Nothing to do with the icy air. My plane will be very easy to spot from above. I swallow, even though my mouth is dry. I remember Dad saying the most important thing you can do in an emergency is stay calm. He didn't say whether that rule applies if there are three emergencies, or even four, one after the other.

'When the sun rises, I have to go. No one knows I'm here. They will be worried,' he says.

My heart thumps in my chest.

'But what should I do? I don't even know where I am. I need to call the police. I need to call my mum. I—' I feel the sob rising in my chest again. How can he be so matter-of-fact after everything that's just happened?

'When we get to my village, then maybe I can help you.'

I try to take in what the boy is saying.

'You'll be able to call the police. Let them know what's happened.'

He's offering to help me.

I take a deep breath.

'Can you walk?' I ask.

The boy smiles. 'I feel much better. I'm just tired,' he adds.

'Is your village nearby?'

'Not too far,' he says. 'If you have a snowmobile.'

I remember arriving at the hut. It looked deserted.

I would have noticed a snowmobile, or snowmobile tracks.

'I have one,' he adds. 'I just need to find it.' I must look confused. 'There was a white-out,' he says. 'I lost my way, and I lost my snowmobile. If the visibility is good, then I'll know where to go.'

'But it all looks the same out there,' I say.

He shakes his head. 'People always think that. People who don't know this land. Just because it's not covered in roads and houses. We should leave here at sunrise. It will be very cold still, but it will give us more time. Do you have everything you need from the plane?'

'Yes, all the bags and the emergency kit too.'

He has gone from hypothermic to expedition planner in the space of an hour.

He looks over at the pile of stuff on the floor and opens his mouth as if he's about to speak, then stops himself. After a moment, he says, 'My name is Yutu. What's yours?'

'I'm Bea, short for Beatrice,' I say.

I wait for him to react in some way, but he doesn't. He just rubs his legs again, then pushes the rugs to one side. When he stands up, his head almost touches the ceiling. He stretches, then picks up his ski trousers and hangs them from the back of the door. He tips his right boot upside down to empty out the rest of the water.

'I think tomorrow I will need to wear a plastic bag on my foot,' he says. He catches my expression. 'Inside my boot. To stop my sock getting wet.'

He picks up one of the rugs and lays it across a raised platform which spans half the hut. I don't know why I didn't notice it before. He picks up the blanket and the other rug and lays them on top.

'We have a very early start tomorrow, so I think we need to get some sleep. It's warmer if we sleep on this,' he says, patting the platform.

'I guess,' I start slowly, 'some of my dad's clothes might fit you.'

He looks over at me but says nothing.

I unzip one of the bags and pass a bundle of clothes to Yutu. While he puts on a few dry layers, I look in the other bag for my hat and an extra jumper.

'I almost feel warm again,' Yutu says, pulling on a second pair of socks. 'Thank you. We should both get under the rug, before it gets any colder. It's caribou skin. It will trap our body heat.'

The rug is surprisingly soft.

'I'll wake you at first light,' says Yutu, and then rolls over with his back towards me.

I switch the torch off. I notice the sounds of the wind, gently whistling across the tundra. The hut creaks. The rhythm is reassuring. My nose is cold, but I am warm beneath the caribou skins. I try to picture Dad, sleeping in a bed somewhere, but the image of him lying on the floor, unconscious, appears instead. I think about Mum, at home. I wonder if she even knows that anything is wrong. Who will tell her? I want to get up and pace around, but I know I have to stay beneath these rugs. I can't let my body temperature drop. I need some rest. I need to sleep.

Kit

'What's in the bags, Bea?'

My eyes flick open. It's dark. I'm cold. The air is icy on my face. I try desperately to remember where I am.

I turn towards the voice and see a tall figure moving around in the gloom.

I remember what happened yesterday. My dad. The two men. Yutu.

I feel around for my torch and switch it on.

Yutu is by the door. He's already in his snow boots. Next to him is the pile of luggage I took from the plane.

'It's just clothes, and stuff for the weekend,' I say. My voice sounds hoarse.

'Is there anything we can leave behind?'

I push the caribou skin to one side.

'Here.' Yutu passes me my boots. 'Put them on while your feet are still warm.'

I go through the bags, taking one set of warm

clothes from each. The clothes smell of home. Of a different Bea.

Yutu flips open the clasps on the emergency kit and examines the packages, taking them out one by one. 'Waterproof matches, emergency blanket, whistle, compass.' He lifts out a second layer. 'Folding water bottle, fishing line and hooks, dried food. Wow,' says Yutu. 'Your dad travels prepared.'

I nod. I don't trust myself to speak without my voice cracking up completely.

I don't like him going through my things. Dad's things.

'How about in that one?' He points to the lunch bag.

I snatch it and put it on my lap.

He glances at me in surprise.

I need to calm down. I need to remember that he's helping me.

I empty everything onto the caribou skin. There are sandwiches, bananas, power bars and some cake. 'Let's share it out,' I say.

Yutu smiles. 'I am so hungry,' he says. 'We should eat something now. It's important to eat a lot when it's cold. Your body needs to burn more energy to keep you warm.' He picks up a banana. 'We don't get many of these,' he says.

'So does everyone from your village hunt for seals?' I ask, trying to sound friendly.

Yutu frowns a little. 'Not everyone,' he says. 'There are *some* other things to do,' he smiles.

'I meant, does everyone know how to?' I say, my cheeks burning in the cold air.

'They used to,' he says. 'Not so much now. My friends prefer gaming.'

He looks at me, like he's waiting for the next question. I try to think of something to ask. I'm used to being the curiosity, not the conversation starter. He doesn't seem to mind that I say nothing.

'So do all your friends know how to fly?' he says.

I like that he assumes I have friends.

I shake my head.

'My dad works for an oil company. They let him borrow a plane. He's a geologist, so he needs to do aerial surveys sometimes. If he has a chance to fly at weekends, then he takes me with him.'

Yutu looks like he's hanging on my every word.

I think about sitting next to Dad when we go flying. About how we discuss our favourite sandwich fillings and variations in air pressure. About how he makes me feel I can do anything. Then I think about our flight yesterday. It felt like he was barely there with me at all. It's almost like I haven't seen Dad properly for weeks.

'We haven't flown much lately. Dad got really busy at work.'

'Do you think that's why he wanted to bring you with him?'

'That's what he said.'

Yutu watches me. 'The sun will rise soon.' He rolls up the blanket and stows it in the bag.

'What about the caribou skins?' I ask.

'This isn't my hut. They belong to someone else.'

I can't imagine why anyone would ever come here. I don't say that to Yutu.

'Ready?' he asks.

I nod.

Search

The freezing air snatches my breath away.

Yutu also gasps. He is looking at the plane.

'You landed that?' he says.

'Not exactly landed. The wing is broken, I think the wheels, too.'

'No. I meant, it's amazing.'

I can't quite make out his expression, behind the fur on his hood. He walks round to the back of the hut, where the ground is higher and stands there for a few minutes, looking at the patchwork of hills ahead. On the horizon, a blaze of orange creeps upwards to meet the dawn sky.

Yutu turns to me. 'Time to go,' he says.

I nod. He slings the bag over his shoulder and picks up his long stick with a spear at the end.

'Stay close to me,' he says. 'There might be snow-drifts or rifts just beneath the surface. We need to follow the coastline.'

I crunch through the snow a few metres behind him, running a little to keep up. The layers of clothing and thick boots make it hard to walk.

Yutu seems to know where he is going.

However hard I stare, I can't see the shape of the coastline, or any particular shapes at all. The land just seems to roll up and down, with dark patches where the snow has blown off the rocks, and small humps which might be trees. There are no buildings to break the horizon. No sounds apart from the wind and the crunching of our feet. No snowmobile. I've never been so far from a town. So far from people.

Yutu walks with a steady rhythm, like he's on autopilot. Finding the flattest ground takes all my concentration. After about ten minutes my legs begin to ache. I notice that we are following some kind of ridge. I can't see what lies beyond it.

Without warning, Yutu stops right in front of me. I bump into the bag slung over his back.

'Look!' he says. I scramble to his side, desperate to see what he's pointing at.

The ridge has dropped away. For a minute I stare, then the meaningless shapes beyond it begin to make sense.

'The bay,' says Yutu, still pointing to a wide arc

filled with lumpy ice and darker, flatter patches which might be water.

As the bay magically configures before my eyes, I become aware of a low humming noise. I spin around, trying to work out where it's coming from.

Yutu stands motionless beside me, scanning the horizon.

'Aeroplane,' he says softly.

A wave of panic passes through me.

Yutu slides the bag round so that it's hanging across his front.

'Do you think you can run?' he asks. I nod.

Gripping the bag with his left arm, he sets off.

I scramble after him. As I pick up speed my feet start to slip. The treads on my boots are packed with snow. Before I can slow down my left foot slides away. I tumble forwards to the ground and roll over a few times. My thigh hits something hard beneath the snow. The pain takes my breath away. For a few seconds I lie still, waiting for the pain to ease.

The humming sound has morphed into the throb of an engine. I turn to see the dark line of an aeroplane in the distance. The dark line doesn't move left or right. It is heading straight towards us. I get to my feet and try to catch up with Yutu. My thigh burns with every step.

133

Yutu slows down and waits for me where the path drops more steeply. The drone of the plane drowns out the crunch of my boots through the snow. I begin to slip again but Yutu reaches out his hand. Together we run towards a grove of stunted pine trees. The plane is so close that I can hear the thump of the propellers. Yutu pulls me towards the edge of the thicket, past the snow-crusted branches. He lets go of my hand and dives between the thin trunks, lying flat on his stomach. I dive down beside him and rest my head on the ground. The tallest tree is no higher than Yutu, but layers of snow cling to the thin branches making a dense canopy.

My chest heaves up and down. The noise from the plane vibrates through my body. It must be flying very low. Drifts of powdery snow shiver from the trees as it passes overhead, engines roaring. Yutu reaches out his hand for mine. Through two layers of gloves, I feel the gentle pressure.

I start counting. After twenty seconds, the plane will be a kilometre away. Too far to see us. But when I reach five seconds, the pitch of the engine begins to change.

'It's coming back,' I say, panic rising in my chest.

The rumble of the engine gets louder, and I fight the urge to run.

I feel Yutu squeeze my hand again. 'They can't land here,' he shouts.

The plane roars past for a second time. I start counting. When I reach thirty, the engine noise has faded to a low humming noise.

I become aware of the chill seeping through my clothes.

'Are you OK?' Yutu's voice draws me back to the snowy copse.

I sit up and nod.

'Planes don't usually fly down the coast,' he says.

'Or do U-turns in the middle of nowhere,' I add.

We are silent for a few minutes. Neither of us mentions who might have been flying it. We both know.

Yutu says, 'They will have seen your plane.' He is staring at me. His dark eyes flick around my face. 'They probably know you survived the landing, now, too.'

My heart starts to beat a little faster.

'Where is the nearest road?' I ask.

Yutu shakes his head. 'There are no roads up here. Everyone gets around by snowmobile, or aeroplane.'

I feel a glow of relief. Then another thought occurs to me.

'Where is the nearest airport?'

Yutu doesn't say anything for a few seconds.

'My village is the nearest place to land,' he says quietly.

I feel myself breathing more quickly. 'Then I'm trapped out here on the ice?'

Thoughts race through my head. How long can I last out here? Where will I sleep? What will I eat?

'I told you before,' he says. 'It's not *I*, it's *we*. I'm not leaving you here. We just need to get to my village before they do,' says Yutu calmly. 'If they're not from the area, it will take time to work out where we might be heading. They will need clearance to fly, too.'

I feel tears pool at the bottom of my eyes, instantly chilled by the icy air. I blink them away.

My mind races. 'If there are no roads for miles around, what will happen when we get to your village? Won't we be trapped there instead?'

Yutu looks at me anxiously.

'We don't have any choice. There's nowhere else,' he pauses, 'and I need to go home. People will be worried about me. I was supposed to return yesterday.'

I bite my lip. I'd forgotten about Yutu disappearing. That people will be wondering where he is.

I think about home. About Mum, alone with Hester, waiting for a message from Dad to say we have arrived safely.

'That sounds like a good plan,' I hesitate, before adding, 'I'm sorry. I didn't think about your mum and dad. Of course, they will be worried.'

'My mum and dad died when I was little,' he says. 'My grandmother will be waiting for me.'

Yutu starts fiddling with his boot, tugging at the plastic bag which pokes out of the top. I just assumed Yutu's family was like mine, without bothering to ask.

After a few moments Yutu looks up. 'We should get going,' he says, pushing himself to his feet. Rather than leaving the spinney the same way we entered, he walks his way into the middle of the thicket, then stops. He is staring at something in a small clearing. I push through the branches and follow his gaze to a snow-covered lump attached to some skis.

'My snowmobile,' says Yutu, turning to me with a smile.

Race

The engine growls into life first time.

A flicker of hope stirs in my stomach.

Yutu beckons. 'Climb on!' he shouts. 'If you need something, tap me on the shoulder.'

'OK,' I yell back.

He presses the accelerator and I jerk backwards, grabbing his coat to stop myself falling.

We glide across the snow, an icy wind pushing against my face. After a few minutes my cheeks are numb. I try to tug my zip a bit higher. At the same time, we drive over a bump and my other hand slips from Yutu's waist. I feel myself tip back. Instantly he slows down, which has the effect of pushing me forwards again. We come to a stop, the engine idling rhythmically.

'It's best not to move around too much,' Yutu shouts. 'Makes it difficult to steer. And you might fall off.'

'You could have told me that before I nearly fell off,' I shout back.

We start to move again, gradually gathering speed.

I cling on more tightly.

As we race through the tundra, the flicker of hope grows. Still no aeroplane.

I notice we are following the soft curve of the shore, beyond which lie lumpy peaks of sea ice. After a while, Yutu steers inland. Hills rise and fall, some smooth, others with wind-blown patches of dark rock at the peak. Between them, flatter ground makes natural pathways. Perhaps it doesn't all look the same.

After an hour or so, I spot a shape ahead, slightly darker than the hill behind, but not dark enough to be rock.

As we get closer, I see it's some kind of hut, in better condition to the one where I found Yutu.

He slows to a stop a few metres away and switches off the engine. My ears ring in the silence. They have grown accustomed to the relentless buzz.

Yutu climbs down and stamps his feet.

'My cabin,' he says, nodding towards the hut. 'Well, my grandmother's cabin. We can have a quick break here. Something to eat and drink.'

He walks around the hut a few times. I see that the

front of his coat and the fur around his jacket have a thin layer of ice on them.

'Someone has been here,' he says.

'How do you know?'

'Tracks in the snow. Another snowmobile.' I look at him in alarm. 'They're not here now,' he adds quickly. 'There are tracks which arrive, and tracks which leave.'

I feel my heart racing.

'Are you sure they've gone?'

He turns to look at me. Without warning, he smiles. 'I think it was someone looking for me, not you,' he says. 'Someone from my village, come to see where I've got to.'

'Oh,' I say, taking a deep breath of cold air.

He unclips a bag from the back of the snowmobile, and rummages around inside.

'Here,' he says, passing me a small lump of something. 'Eat this.'

I take a bite. It has a texture like fudge but leaves a greasy feel on my lips. It tastes a bit like fish.

'What is it?' I ask, putting my hand out for the second piece he offers.

'Seal fat.'

I feel the saliva rise in my mouth. I stare at the lump of fat on my glove.

'What's the matter?' says Yutu.

'I just—I like seals,' is all I manage.

'I'm sure I'd like sheep if I ever met one,' he says.

'But sheep are meant to be eaten,' I say.

'Says who?'

'Well, they're bred to be eaten.'

'Poor sheep,' says Yutu. 'This seal was free.'

'Well, yes,' I say, 'they're wild animals.'

'We kill what we need, not what we want.' He looks at me, his expression neutral, but his eyes are flashing with an emotion I don't recognize. 'And now we can't even do that.'

I put the seal meat in my mouth and chew. Wondering what he means.

'You should try this, too.' He passes me a piece of bread with a lump of berries in some kind of butter.

I take a bite. Sweet and sour berries mix with a creamy butter which melts in my mouth.

'What was it?' I ask.

'Cloudberries in seal fat.' He looks at me, the faintest hint of a smile at the corners of his mouth.

He turns to look at the horizon.

Instinctively I whip round, wondering whether he's heard the hum of an aeroplane engine.

The grey-white sky is empty.

'We should go,' he says. 'The days are still short here. But first I need to melt some snow for us to drink.'

'Can't we just put some in our mouths?' I say, surprised.

'It takes a long time to melt a small amount of snow in your mouth. It also cools your body down, which isn't a good idea.'

He disappears into the hut, taking a tiny stove and pan.

I climb off the snowmobile. My legs are very stiff, and my feet are cold. I stamp them, like Yutu did. They tingle painfully.

I follow him inside. Like the first hut, there is a raised area. This one has a neat pile of folded rugs and caribou skins. On a wooden box in the corner are some carved figures. I walk over to look more closely.

'Bone,' says Yutu. 'They're carved from bone.'

Everything is neatly arranged. There is a sweet smell of wood, mixed with something earthy.

When Yutu has finished, we gather up the things and head outside. He slides the bolt back across the door.

I shiver. The hut felt cosy, if cosy applies in sub-zero temperatures.

'Are you warm enough, Bea?' he asks, as he stows the pan and stove.

'I'm OK,' I say. 'How about you?'

He smiles again. 'I only really feel the cold when I've fallen in the sea.' He sighs. 'I'm not looking forward to telling my grandmother what happened. She thought I was staying at my friend's house.'

'Who do you think came to look for you?'

'I'm not sure. Maybe my grandmother's old friend, Petur. He uses our cabin sometimes. He knows the way.' He pauses. 'My grandmother didn't want me to go on my own. I guess she was right.'

'My mum doesn't like me flying,' I say.

'At least she lets you leave town.'

I think about how many towns we've left. How many cities. When I wished we could have stayed.

'We only have a couple of hours of daylight left,' he says, climbing onto the snowmobile. 'Ready?'

Tired

We speed over flat ground, the snowmobile humming. Hills rise and fall on either side. Every few minutes bumps or ridges jerk the whole machine from side to side, turning the hum into an angry buzz. My thighs ache from gripping the seat, and my arms feel weak from clinging to Yutu.

I think about Stella and Becky sitting in class, wondering where I am. Then I realize that it's Sunday. The familiar knot in my stomach begins to tighten, even though Stella and Becky are hundreds of kilometres away. I don't need them here, in the middle of the Arctic. But when I try to push them away, thoughts about Dad creep in. I'm frightened of where they will take me. Every passing minute feels like time wasted until I have some answers. I must find out where he is. I have to help him. My sense of dread grows when I think of him with those men. I feel myself losing control of my fear.

My eyes flick to the endless space, expecting a town or village to appear. I wish my head could share the emptiness around me, instead of crowding with anxieties.

I want to focus on something else. Mum drifts into my head, Mum in the kitten café with her cream moustache. Hester curled up on my bed. I lean further forwards, resting on Yutu's back.

I feel so tired. I have no idea whether we've been driving for one hour or two hours.

The sun sinks to meet the horizon, casting a golden glow across the snow. The hum from the snowmobile makes a kind of white noise, blocking out the thoughts which frighten me.

I fight to keep my eyes open.

Something grabs at my arm. I pull away in panic and see Yutu gripping a chunk of my coat. I am leaning sideways from the snowmobile, my head skimming the ground. I grab his arm and struggle to pull myself upright. The snowmobile rocks from side to side and slides to a stop. Yutu twists right round in his seat and lifts me the rest of the way up. I slump forwards onto his chest and sit like that for a minute, trying to catch my breath, trying not to think about how close I came to being pulled beneath the skis.

There is no humming sound. The engine must have cut out when Yutu took his hands from the accelerator. When I finally sit up, Yutu doesn't look angry, he looks concerned.

'Are you OK?' he asks.

'Yes, I think so. I'm sorry.'

'That's another thing I should have warned you about,' he says. 'It's easy to fall asleep on the back, but not a good idea.'

I nod. 'Is it much further?'

The sky has turned a purplish grey. Dusk is falling.

'We're nearly there,' he says. 'Five minutes.'

He revs the engine.

My stomach twists. I am closer to helping Dad, but also closer to finding out what's happened to him.

After a few minutes I notice a faint yellowish haze up ahead. Perhaps it's the lights from Yutu's village.

He steers in a big arc around the bottom of a steep hill, then slows down so the engine is just ticking over.

A building appears, hidden until the last moment by the curve of the hill. It seems to be made of the land on which it sits. Rocks and moss. It looks like a relic. An ancient building from another age. Yutu drives the snowmobile up alongside. He switches the engine off and climbs down. He sticks out his chest, arching his back in a stretch.

'This is my house,' he says in a low voice. 'I need to go in first, to speak to my grandmother. To explain. To let her know you are here.'

He walks towards a small doorway, barely visible in the gloom.

Home

After a few minutes, Yutu hasn't returned. The sun has set, and the temperature is dropping rapidly. I was cold when we arrived. Now I'm shivering.

I hesitate before knocking on the door. It makes a warm, hollow sound. Yutu answers. Behind him is a small lady with white hair, neatly braided. She is looking at me with a mixture of shock and surprise.

'Who is this?' she asks.

'This is Bea, Grandma.'

She beckons me inside. She isn't smiling. I'm used to people not smiling at me.

'Please have a seat,' Yutu says. There are only two, and his grandmother has gone to sit in one of them, so I sit down next to her. She is still staring at me. I can no longer tell if her expression is one of shock, or curiosity, or both.

She turns to Yutu. 'You need to tell me what happened,' she says. 'Now, Yutu.'

I thought Yutu's grandmother would be friendlier. More like him. Perhaps it's because she's been worried about him. Parents have a habit of seeming cross when they're worried. I guess it must apply to grandparents too.

Yutu collects a small stool from the corner of the room. It's smooth and creamy-white, like the bone figures in his cabin. He places it a few metres in front of the chairs. He's too big for it. When he sits down his knees rise up, so he has no choice but to rest his elbows on them.

He licks his lips and begins to talk. Yutu looks younger when he's speaking to his grandmother. He tells her that she was right. There were no seals in the bay. He tells her that Petur was right too, it's because the water is too warm. The sea ice was melting, even though it's early spring. He describes the storm closing in and the white-out. His grandmother lifts her hand to her forehead and closes her eyes.

It's the first time I've heard the whole story of how Yutu came to be in the hut. How Yutu managed to pull himself out of the sea ice and walk half-frozen through the blizzard.

'That's where Bea found me. I had hypothermia. She gave me blankets and dry clothes. She gave me something warm to drink.'

He looks over at me and I realize that I'm staring. Wisps of hair which have escaped from my hood are defrosting. I brush away the melted ice as it drips down the side of my face.

Yutu's grandmother nods slowly, then starts talking to him in a language I don't understand. Even though she spoke English when I arrived.

She doesn't seem to ask him anything about what happened. She seems to be telling him something. Her tone is steady and serious.

Yutu frowns. His expression changes to one of disbelief. He looks over at me.

I want to know what's happening.

Yutu's grandmother turns to me. 'Thank you for looking after my grandson,' she says. 'He was very lucky that you were there to help him. Reckless behaviour doesn't usually end well.'

I smile at her. I'm about to say that Yutu rescued me, too, but she's already turned back to speak to him.

Then she gets up and walks slowly towards the front door.

Yutu leaps up. 'No!' he says. 'Please wait.'

Something is very wrong.

'What's going on?' I ask.

Before his grandmother can slip her coat on, Yutu is by her side. He seems to be pleading with her. Then he takes her gently by the arm and leads her back to her chair. She places her coat on her knees.

'Please tell my grandmother what happened to you, Bea.' There is a look of desperation in Yutu's eyes. 'She wants to hear about why you were out on the ice on your own. She needs to hear it from you.'

His grandmother is looking at me. She still doesn't smile, but there is a warmth in her eyes which wasn't there when I first arrived. I don't know what's going on, but I can sense that Yutu is trying to help me. That I need to do this.

His grandma listens in silence while I describe leaving home on Saturday morning, then arriving at the airport, where the men were waiting for my dad. She says nothing, but I notice her shake her head, almost imperceptibly, when I describe flying the plane across the tundra, by myself.

When I've finished, she is staring ahead, like she's thinking.

'What you did takes courage,' she says. 'You didn't give up, even though giving up might have been easier.' She pauses. 'You must be hungry. Let me get you something to eat, then we can talk a little more.'

'Thank you,' I say. 'But first I would really like to call my mum. She hasn't heard from me since yesterday morning. I need to speak to the police too, or maybe Mum will do that.'

She nods slowly, then says something to Yutu.

'I wish I knew what you were saying,' I say quietly. I'm starting to feel so tired. Like I just want to go to sleep until it's all over.

His grandma gets up and walks towards the kitchen area. Halfway there, she turns to Yutu and says, 'Tell her, then.'

Yutu looks pale.

'Tell me what?' I say.

'Bea,' he says, then hesitates, like he's not sure how to begin. 'Grandma says that there's been a message. The mayor had a phone call. It was someone who said they were from the police.'

I feel my blood run cold.

What could this possibly have to do with my dad?

'They are looking for a girl. They have reason to believe she might be lost somewhere out on the tundra. They said that if we find her, we must keep her safe and warm until they can come and collect her. They said her father has been arrested. He was trying to leave the country with sensitive corporate information and was using his daughter as a cover. They captured him, but she escaped in a plane. She may be injured. She is likely to be very distressed. She probably doesn't know what her father has done, and so we shouldn't discuss it with her.'

I feel myself shaking my head slowly.

'Whoever called the mayor is lying,' I say, breathing quickly. I try to stay calm, to think about what is going on, but my head is spinning. 'Is this what you were talking about? Were you deciding whether or not to tell me?'

'Grandma was explaining what had happened,' says Yutu.

'It's the men who attacked my dad. Can't you see? They're making sure I'm trapped until they get here. They won't want me to talk to anybody. I escaped before, and they don't want to risk it happening again.'

Yutu's grandmother says something to him.

'What?' I say to Yutu. 'Please, tell me what you're saying.'

'She said, what if you simply don't know what your father has done, like the message said.'

I feel a sob building inside me. I feel helpless.

'I know what I saw. My dad was attacked. You believe me, don't you?'

'Yes,' he says. 'She wants to figure out what's going on. Just like you do.'

'There's nothing to figure out,' I say. 'Some men attacked my dad. I don't know who they were. I don't know why they did it. But it seems they don't want anyone else to know either.'

There is a loud knock at the door.

Yutu rushes over to my chair. 'Go to one of the rooms at the back,' he whispers. I stare at him, confused. 'Go, quickly,' he says, steering me towards two open doors hidden in the shadows. I pick one which leads to a bedroom, as his grandmother goes to answer the door.

I hear conversation, and a man's voice. After a few minutes I hear the door open and close again.

'Bea,' Yutu calls.

I walk towards the sitting room and wait in the shadows.

'Who was that?' I ask.

'It was someone from the village. They wanted to see if I'd come home. It would be best if no one knew you were here—for now.'

I move slowly from the shadows, towards Yutu.

I realize that I'm trembling.

'He must have heard me,' I say quietly. 'He must know I'm here.'

'Maybe not,' Yutu says. 'The walls are very thick.'

I sit on the nearest chair and close my eyes. I feel a tear roll down my cheek. I'm too tired to brush it away.

Yutu picks up the stool and sits with me. I can hear his grandma moving about by the stove.

'You've never met my dad,' I say, 'you don't know what he's like. But you know me. A little bit, anyway. My dad would never steal. Not secrets, not anything. You don't have to believe me, but please don't try to stop me from helping him. Why would someone do this?'

'Can I ask you a question?' Yutu says quietly. 'What does a geologist who works for an oil company do?'

I close my eyes. This doesn't feel like the right time to explain petroleum geology.

'Your dad was on a work trip,' he adds. 'Maybe if I know more about what he does, we can find a clue to what's going on, to who might have wanted your dad to disappear.'

'Is your grandma going to tell the mayor I'm here?' I ask.

'She's making soup. A good sign. But you can never rush Grandma.'

I take a deep breath. 'He finds new oil and gas reserves. He helps companies work out how to get to it.'

'So it's an important job?' he asks.

'Every oil company wants him to work for them.'

'Why?'

'I guess because he's really good. He makes them a lot of money.'

He thinks for a minute. Then looks at me, his eyes bright.

'What if—' he begins. 'What if those men were trying to kidnap your dad?'

I look at him, confused. 'But why?'

'If he's so valuable to his company, then maybe they'd pay a ransom for his release.'

'Then why would they say he's stealing company secrets? It doesn't make sense.'

Yutu nods. 'You're right. Is there anything else, anything at all, which you think might be a clue, might be important?'

His grandma is still preparing something by the stove, but I can tell she is listening.

'Well,' I try to think. I'm so tired. 'Dad has been working really hard for the last couple of weeks, on some big project. He seemed pretty stressed. He doesn't normally get stressed about anything.' I pause for a moment. 'I guess it was unusual for him to take me on a work trip. He's never done that before. But I wasn't having the best time at school. Maybe he thought it would do me some good.'

I think back to when we landed. I force myself to replay what I saw when I looked through the window.

Then I remember what I heard. 'My dad said something about lying,' I say.

'To you?' Yutu asked.

'No, I heard him say it to one of the men. They were shouting at him. Then when I was inside the aeroplane, Dad came out of the building. He yelled at me to go, to take off. He would never have told me to do that if I would have been safer on the ground.'

Yutu's grandmother wipes her hands, then goes to her bedroom.

A few moments later she returns with something in her hand. She passes it to me. It's her phone. It's one of the old ones which only does dialling and texting.

'If we're going to sort this out, I think it's time to call your mum,' she says.

I clutch the phone, my heart thumping again. I try to remember our new number. I tap it in and after a few seconds, it starts to ring.

'Hello?' Mum sounds anxious.

'Mum, it's Bea,' I say.

There is a short silence.

'Bea, darling, are you OK? I've been so worried.' She knows something is wrong.

'I'm OK, Mum. I'm fine. But, Mum, something's happened.' I swallow, preparing to tell her about the men at the airport.

Before I can begin, Mum says, 'I know that Dad's in trouble, Bea. We can help him.'

'Really? You know what happened?'

'There's someone here with me now—from the police.'

That's what she meant by 'we'.

'They will come and get you,' she says, 'then we can sort everything out.'

Someone takes the phone.

'Bea?' It's a man's voice. 'I need you to stay calm and stay where you are. Bea, can you hear me?'

I press the red button to end the call. I sit very still, the phone resting in my hand.

'What happened?' Yutu says.

'There was a man there with Mum. Mum said they needed to speak to me. That something serious had happened. It sounds like the same message that your mayor got. They took the phone from her, to talk to me, so I hung up.'

I close my eyes. There is no question now. I'm trapped.

Soup

I am curled up in a chair, my knees tucked towards my chin. I feel weak with hunger. My body aches from hours on the snowmobile. Yutu's grandma carries two bowls over from the stove, steam snaking round her face. All I can manage is to uncurl my legs and take the bowl which she offers. She passes the other to Yutu, perched on his stool.

'Time to eat,' she says. 'Whatever you are feeling now, will be a little bit better when you have some food in your stomach.'

She passes me a spoon.

'Thank you—'

'My name is Miki. When you've finished, then we can talk about how to get you home.'

I lift a spoonful of soup to my mouth. Golden pools of fat shimmer on the top. It's rich and warm.

Miki sits down next to me, her hands in her lap. Silently, peacefully, she watches me and Yutu as we eat. I feel no pressure to fill the silence. Each spoon-ful of soup melts a little of my panic, thaws the chill from hours spent outside.

As I wait for the soup to cool, I look around the room, at the amber-coloured wood on the walls and floor, at the stove and sink in the corner, the old chest beneath the window. It's peaceful, like Miki. There is a kind of harmony between the objects. Each has a purpose, a place. There is a sense of calm, of homeliness.

Miki brings a small bowl of the berry mix to share, then settles down, with a cup of her sweet-smelling tea.

'Was the soup good?' she asks.

'It was delicious,' I say.

She nods, unsurprised by my answer.

'Now I think we can talk.' Miki takes a few sips of tea, and leans forwards in her chair, towards me and Yutu. 'We are far from big towns and cities here, Bea. Separated by snow and ice or by rivers and mountains. All year round there are planes, but only for deliver-ies or emergencies. In summer and autumn, you can travel the coast by boat. In winter you can travel on the sea ice.' She sighs. 'But now, it's spring. I'm afraid you can't do either of those. The ice isn't solid, but it hasn't melted either. To reach the nearest big town you would have to travel overland. From there you can take the sleeper train anywhere you want.'

'But isn't that what we were doing all the way back from the cabin—travelling overland?'

'Yes, but you would be going further, and Yutu has only travelled the route once before.'

Yutu sits up straight on his stool, like something's bitten him.

'You'd let me take Bea?' he says, his eyes wide. 'Along the south-coast route?'

'I haven't forgiven you for running away,' says Miki.

'I didn't run away—'

'I haven't forgiven you, but you and Bea are a good team. A good team can make up for inexperience. Sometimes.'

'I promise I wouldn't do anything reckless, just exactly what you say.' Yutu's words tumble out, until Miki raises her hand, a faint smile on her lips.

'Yutu, going overland is hard. It's dangerous. There will be no one to help you if there is a problem.' She pauses. 'And it's not my decision alone. Bea must choose.'

I don't think I've missed anything, but so far I've only heard one option. 'If I don't go overland, then what would I do?'

Miki turns to me. 'You would have to wait for a

delivery plane. It will probably be a couple of weeks before the next one. Then maybe you could hitch a flight back.'

I look from Miki to Yutu. For me the choice is clear. 'Overland.'

The skin around Miki's eyes crinkles as she smiles back. 'I trust you, Bea. When you talk about what happened to your father, you speak from your heart,' she says. Her expression is steady and serene. 'I believe helping you is the right thing to do.'

I don't know what time it is. Not long after we ate soup, but I'm so tired. Layers of blanket and thick caribou skin press gently against me. I feel my eyes closing. Thoughts buzz nearby, vying for attention, but they can't take hold.

I hear something. At first, I think I'm dreaming, then I realize it's Yutu's voice.

I open my eyes. He's standing by the door.

He leans over and passes me a small scrap of paper.

'This was in the pocket of your dad's trousers. I didn't want to throw it away.'

'Thank you,' I murmur. I close my hand around the piece of paper. Whatever it is can wait until the morning.

Share

I stare at the honey-coloured ceiling glowing in the morning light. At the pattern of swirling knots and wavy lines. Miki's bed is empty, the covers pulled up neatly. The herby smell of her tea drifts into the room. I want to lie here for a minute longer. My nose and cheeks are cold. I'm glad I slept in my clothes. It won't feel so cold when I push the warm covers away.

There is something in my hand. A small piece of paper. I half-remember Yutu giving it to me before I fell asleep. I sit up, and unfold the scrap, smoothing it flat in the palm of my hand. Written in black biro, are the words *Tell Bea—Hester*. It's Dad's handwriting, but I have no idea what he would want to tell me about Hester.

'Bea, would you like some breakfast?' Yutu calls from the other side of the bedroom door. I fold up the paper and slip it into my pocket.

'Coming,' I answer.

Miki is pottering by the stove.

'Sleep well?' she asks.

'I think I slept well,' I say. 'The caribou skin was so warm. I like the smell.'

Miki smiles. I realize she is looking at my clothes. I'm wearing a jumper, two fleeces and several pairs of socks.

She walks over to the old wooden chest on the floor by her chair. She pokes around inside and then passes me a pair of slippers. '*Ilupirquk*,' she says. 'Handmade. Put them on.'

I look at the shape, the beautiful stitches.

I tug them on. The soft leather moves with my foot, almost like a sock. I look up at Miki. 'They're beautiful.'

'My mother taught me to sew. Her mother taught her.'

'I see my grandparents once a year,' I say. 'We are always in a different country. What else do you make? May I see?'

Miki goes back to the chest and takes out some mittens.

'Sealskin,' she says, passing them to me. 'Nothing goes to waste. The blubber we use to light lamps, the bones for needles, and the rest we eat.'

I slip my hands inside.

'How do you make them so soft?' I ask.

'We scrape the leather,' says Miki. 'People used to chew the leather too, to soften it.'

I pass them back to Miki. '*Naormeek*,' I say.

She stares at me, beaming. 'You speak our language?'

I laugh. 'No, no. I just worked out the word for thank you from listening to you and Yutu. I like learning languages.'

'You spoke it perfectly,' Miki says.

She slips on her coat and heads towards the door. 'I'm going to the cold store,' she says to no one in particular. A few moments later she returns, clutching a small package.

Kneeling on the floor by my chair, she peels away several paper layers. Inside lies a block of something reddish-brown. Using a sharp knife, Miki shaves a thin slice and passes it to me.

'Is that caribou?' Yutu asks. 'I thought we didn't have any?'

'Just a little bit saved,' Miki says. 'I thought Bea might like to try it.'

'It's raw.' Yutu adds, 'It has quite a strong flavour.'

It has a salty, earthy taste. I like it. 'Mmm,' I say.

Miki's face crinkles in delight.

Yutu shakes his head and smiles. 'Only for special visitors,' he says.

Miki cuts a slice for Yutu and for herself.

'You're jealous. Normally you have all the best pieces to yourself. It's good for you to share. Do you have brothers or sisters, Bea?' she asks.

'No, just Mum and Dad and Hester.'

'Hester?'

'My cat.'

She nods. 'Yutu has no brother or sister. But at least you have your mother and father. He just has an old woman for company.'

She passes me another slice. 'This is what's left from last autumn's hunt,' talking to me as if Yutu is no longer here.

'I like the idea of living from the land.'

'It's not an idea,' Miki says. 'It's the way we live.'

I feel my cheeks flush.

As we finish the last few chunks of bread, I become aware of a low whining sound.

I look over at Yutu. 'What's that?'

The noise gets louder and deeper.

Yutu jumps to his feet. 'Stay here,' he says. He pulls on his boots and heads out of the door.

I rush to the small window and peer through the thick glass. I can't see anything, but the sound is unmistakable now. An aeroplane.

Fear

The door creaks open. Yutu hurries in, pink-cheeked.

'I made it round the hill in time. I saw the plane coming into land.'

'What did it look like?' I ask quietly.

'Silver, with a red mark down the side.'

The same as Dad's plane. The same as the plane at the airport. I feel my heart thump in my chest.

'It's them.'

'How do you know?' Yutu asks.

'Silver and red. It has to be them.'

'It looked like a four-seater,' says Yutu. 'Too small to be a delivery.'

My thoughts spin. 'How long will it take them to get to the village?'

'The landing strip is about five hundred metres to the south, so about fifteen minutes to the edge of town. Grandma's house is a bit further. Another five or ten minutes.'

'You have to leave. Now.'

Yutu and I both turn to look at Miki. She is still kneeling on the floor. Her expression is calm, her chin slightly raised, her lips unsmiling. She is serious.

I remember what Miki said yesterday. It would be a dangerous journey. There would be no one to help if we had a problem.

'But we haven't got anything ready,' I say. 'We haven't prepared.'

'There is no time,' says Miki. 'News travels fast in our village. It won't take long to find out where you're hiding, Bea.'

I think about the man knocking on Miki's door last night.

'We don't need much,' says Yutu. 'Warm clothes, stove, emergency kit. The things we had with us before.'

I head to the bedroom and throw everything in my bag. I'm already wearing most of my clothes.

We start piling things on the floor by the chairs. Most of it is still packed from when we arrived last night. Yutu appears with some extra trousers and jumpers. Miki adds some packages and a round tin filled with bannock bread. She disappears to her bedroom for a minute. When she returns, she is holding a small sealskin wallet.

'Money,' she says, passing it to Yutu. He tries to give it back. 'Take it. You'll need something when you get there.'

I sense the seconds ticking by. There is no window at the back of the house. No escape route if someone knocks on the door.

Miki takes Yutu's hand, straight-backed and composed, yet her head barely reaches his shoulder.

'You know where to join the way south, but the path isn't always clear. When you are close to the big river, you will see two peaks. Pass them, and the town is only an hour away.'

Yutu nods. 'I remember. What about Sami?' he says.

Miki looks at him blankly.

'We're using his snowmobile.'

She makes a soft sighing sound. 'He lent you that snowmobile when he should have gone with you, instead. I will speak to his father. They have a snowmobile each in that family. They can spare one.'

Yutu leans his head to one side, like he's never considered this.

I look anxiously towards the door. Twenty minutes must have passed since the plane landed.

'If someone comes looking, I will tell them that you went back to the cabin,' Miki says.

'Why would I go back to the cabin?'

'Perhaps to look for the girl?' Grandma shrugs. 'I have to tell them something. The cabin is in the opposite direction to the way you are going. It doesn't matter if they believe me. It's better than telling them where you've really gone.'

Yutu bends down, and Miki presses her nose to his cheek, like she's breathing him in.

We scoop up the bags and packages from the floor.

'Wait,' says Miki. She goes over to the wooden chest. 'If you borrow someone's cabin, then it's right to leave a gift.' She passes Yutu a pair of mittens. 'Something easy to carry.' She holds out a second pair. 'Bea, these are for you,' she says.

'*Naormeek*,' I say. She puts out her arms and I hug her. When I move away, her eyes are sparkling.

'*Tavauvuteet*,' says Yutu. 'Goodbye.'

I wonder if what we're about to do counts as courage or recklessness.

Brave

Yutu speeds past mounds of dark rock blown clean by the wind. We're going faster than yesterday. He steers between the collage of hillocks and drifts, miraculously finding a way. We lean into a corner without slowing down. I grip his waist, making sure my body doesn't unbalance the machine and tip us over. Snow flicks up on either side. The roar of the engine seems outrageously loud after the peace of Miki's house. It feels like the whole village must know exactly where we are, but we're hidden from view behind a low, wide hill that sweeps around the bay in a horseshoe.

Wind pushes against my nose and cheeks. It sneaks beneath the fur on my hood. My face is cold, but it doesn't chill my whole body in the way it did yesterday. I have slept and eaten. My hands are warm inside the sealskin gloves which Miki gave me.

I try to picture her now, sitting calmly in her chair, waiting. A flicker of fear spreads through my chest when I imagine those men stepping inside her home. Asking Miki if she knows anything which might help them. She will give nothing away. But she is doing this for me, also a stranger. When I needed help, she shared her house and made me feel like family.

Then I think about the man who visited Mum. Who was it? Surely the men who attacked Dad couldn't fly there and back in time. Does that mean there are others involved? I wish I could have spoken to her properly. I wonder what they've told her. Whether she knows about me flying the plane. Whether they told her the same things they told the mayor in Yutu's village. Anger flares inside me again when I think about them describing Dad stealing secrets from work. Taking important information so that he can sell it. As quickly as it arrived, my anger fades, replaced with something else. Something I try to push away. Ignore. Because I know what it is, and it's too awful to face. The thing is a flicker of doubt. A flicker of doubt about whether Dad was hiding something. I squeeze my arms more tightly around Yutu.

'Are you OK?' he shouts.

'Yes,' I shout back. 'All OK.'

I try to focus on the pale blue sky, the sun sparkling on the snow. As we pass the lower slopes of the horseshoe hill, a new vista unfolds. A rolling ocean of small peaks, grey shadows highlighting the white tips. Yesterday it would have seemed desolate and empty. Today it feels peaceful. Safe. It's also beautiful.

Just as my arms feel too weak to cling on, Yutu steers towards a rocky outcrop. We slow to a stop in the shadow cast beneath, and I realize it offers a natural shelter from the wind. Yutu climbs slowly off and stamps his feet.

'Time for a break,' he says. We must have been driving for a couple of hours. 'I need to check the route.'

I climb off and try to stamp my feet too, but my legs feel so stiff I have to stand still for a few minutes first.

'Do you need to check the compass?' I ask.

Yutu smiles and slowly shakes his head. He looks around at the snow by his feet. I wonder if he's dropped something when he says, 'Look,' pointing to a lump of ice.

'What?' I ask.

'The ice tells me which way to go.'

I push my hood back a little to look at him properly.

'Have you been driving for too long without a break?'

He smiles again. 'If the wind blows from the west, it makes these peaks in the ice. So they always point east.'

'But doesn't the wind change direction all the time?'

'No. It normally blows from the east or the west. When it blows from the east the snow makes a different shape.'

I shake my head. 'I know about using the sun and the stars to navigate. I had no idea you could use snow and wind. My dad would love this,' I say, feeling a twist inside as I wonder when I will speak to him again. As I wonder where he is.

Then I remember the note.

I pull off my mitten.

Yutu watches anxiously.

Cold bites at my fingers as I feel in my pocket for the scrap of paper.

'Is that the piece of paper I found?' he asks.

I nod and pass it to him.

'Tell Bea—Hester.' He looks up, his dark brown eyes searching my face for an answer.

'It's my dad's handwriting.'

'But isn't Hester your cat?'

I sigh. 'Yes. What would Dad want to tell me about her? It doesn't make any sense.'

He reaches over to unzip one of the bags at the back of the snowmobile. He pulls out a chunk of bread then tears it in two and hands a piece to me. 'Eat this,' he says. 'No one ever had a good idea on an empty stomach.'

'Who said that?' I ask.

'Me,' says Yutu.

As he chews the bread he stares across the tundra towards the horizon.

'Do you make this bread in a frying pan?' I ask, remembering Miki cooking some yesterday.

I think Yutu heard me, but he doesn't turn his head. He's staring intently, not at the horizon.

'Keep still,' he whispers.

An icy chill runs down my spine.

'Over there, by the patch of rock.'

I follow his eyes, but all I can see is the patch of rock, then I see something move nearby.

'What is it?' I whisper.

'Arctic fox,' he says.

I lose sight of it, then the fox lifts its head to sniff the air. Its fur is white, and almost impossible to distinguish from the snow.

'How does it survive here? I mean, what does it eat? Everything's frozen.'

Yutu looks at me and tilts his head to one side.

'They adapt,' he says. 'It takes time, and then they pass the knowledge on. Arctic foxes teach their cubs how to hunt in the snow, where to sleep. Then the cubs grow up and teach their cubs.' A moment passes, then he adds, 'Just like people adapt.'

I think of the soft gloves which Miki gave me, and how much warmer they are than my thermal gloves from the mountaineering shop. How her mother taught her how to sew them, and her mother before.

'I didn't mean—'

'Don't worry,' says Yutu. 'People find it hard to understand our way of life sometimes, our traditions. The land shapes us. Not the other way round. The land, the weather, the animals who share it with us. There is a balance.'

I like listening to Yutu. The way he talks is different from the boys at school. He makes me think.

'We should get moving,' he says. 'There is still a long way to go.'

I finish the last piece of bread and wait while Yutu unclips the fuel canister from the back of the snowmobile and carefully fills the tank. He secures the empty can beneath the bags and we climb on.

Yutu revs the engine and we slide into the patchwork of icy hills, stretching as far as the eye can see.

The sunlight becomes watery as grey-blue clouds gather along the horizon. After an hour or so, it's no more than a yellowish glow. I can't figure out where the sky ends and the land begins. Yutu slows as we approach a steep hill with patches of rough ice beneath, frozen into peaks a metre high. He climbs off and scrambles a short distance up the hill, looking for a route through. He walks back, shaking his head.

'We have to find another way.'

I can tell that the sun has begun its descent, and there is no sign of the twin mountains to signal we are close to town.

Yutu turns the snowmobile around in a tight circle, and we head back, following our original tracks.

I think about the kilometres of snow and ice between us and anyone who might help if something happened. There is no roadside pick-up. No mobile signal. We haven't passed any cabins, either. If we don't make it as far as the town tonight, then we'll need somewhere to sleep.

On the back of the snowmobile, my fears seem to grow. They might just swallow me up, like the snowy grey landscape.

I try to think about something else, just as the snowmobile begins to slow. We've been retracing our route for about ten minutes. Yutu steers hard to the left and then accelerates to climb a shallow hill which leads to a wide, smooth run of snow. He's found a new route.

I'm desperate to stop and rest again, but I know we must keep going.

The wide path is lined with patches of smooth dark rock. It slopes downwards and Yutu speeds through, swerving to avoid the frozen drifts. If he oversteers and we hit the rocks then we might break one of the skis or worse still, some bones. I cling tightly to his coat and bury my face in its soft fur.

When I peek round his shoulder again, the wind feels colder after the warmth of his coat. Ahead there is some kind of dip in the path. A wave of panic passes through me. On either side of the dip, three or four people have gathered. My heart begins to thump. I tap Yutu on the shoulder but he doesn't seem to notice.

'Yutu!' I shout. He slows down but the hill has given us momentum and we don't stop until the figures are no more than a hundred metres in front.

'OK?' he asks.

I point to the group. Yutu stares ahead but he doesn't react. I wonder if the endless white has started to play tricks with my eyes. Then I hear a noise from within his hood, some kind of gasp. He turns to me.

He doesn't look shocked. He is laughing, his dark brown eyes twinkling.

'You would be a good caribou,' he smiles.

'What?' I say.

'Let's go and say hello.'

He revs the engine. I tug at his hood but we slide onwards to the figures. When we are about twenty metres away, he stops again.

I blink a few times and then look again. There are no people, just piles of rocks, cleverly shaped to look human.

Yutu turns round. He is smiling. It's a kind smile. He doesn't want me to feel stupid, but I do.

'Hunters make these,' he says. 'They build piles of stones near river crossings which the caribou use, so the caribou get spooked and cross further up the river, where it's narrower, and where the real hunters are waiting.'

I close my eyes. 'So these are a decoy?'

'Yes. Animals have routes they prefer, just like humans. Once a hunter learns where the routes are, then they have the advantage.'

'OK,' I nod. 'I would make a good caribou.'

As my fear fades, I realize how cold I am. I rub my hands together.

'Perhaps we should eat a little now,' Yutu says.

He looks at the sky. 'We can't stop for long. There's about an hour of daylight left. We need to find somewhere to spend the night.'

'You don't think we'll make it all the way today?'

Yutu shakes his head. 'We've had to go slowly.'

It didn't feel like we were going slowly. But there is still no sign of the two peaks.

I want to ask where we'll sleep, but I think I know the answer. We have to hope there's a cabin. We eat quickly, then climb back on. My legs ache, made worse by the chill spreading up from my cold feet.

He twists around. 'We're about to cross the river. I need to keep a steady speed as we go over the top. If you hear a noise like gunshot, it's the ice cracking. Don't worry. It will hold us.'

Now I do feel worried. I hold on tightly.

Yutu slides down the bank. I imagine the rumble of caribou hooves as a herd crosses, their bodies jostling together, steaming in the cold air.

We glide across the river and speed up the other side. I feel more awake, but I am still cold. My toes are numb. There is a chill spreading slowly through my body. The clouds are drifting apart to reveal a pinkish sky. A clear sky will mean a colder night. We must find shelter before the temperature begins to plummet.

Freeze

Dusk is falling. The snowy hills have turned dark grey, outlined against a golden horizon. The sky looks strangely warm, but wind is biting through my layers, blowing under my hood. The way ahead is almost impossible to make out. There isn't enough light to drive quickly. I'm sure we should have stopped by now.

I can no longer tell how cold I feel. I'm not even shivering. I would like somewhere to curl up and sleep. With every bump I feel less and less strength in my arms to hold on. I feel my eyes closing.

When I open them again, there is silence. The snowmobile is still. I feel Yutu move in front of me. Holding me up.

'Bea,' he says. 'Bea, are you OK?'

'Cold,' I murmur.

'Bea, don't fall asleep.' I try to open my eyes. Yutu

is holding me under my arms. His face is level with mine. 'Bea, you have to stay awake.'

I know I have to wake up. I know that falling asleep when you're cold is a bad idea. But the wind is freezing and it's dark. I would rather close my eyes again and wait until morning. Somewhere in my half-conscious thoughts, I also know that if I fall asleep morning might not come.

'Bea. Bea!' Yutu is more insistent. I open my eyes. He is frowning. 'We need to get you inside.'

He seems to move round behind me. I feel him lifting me, my feet sliding along the ground. I don't want to move, but I need to help Yutu. We pass through some kind of doorway. On the other side, it's snowy too. It shouldn't be snowy inside. I wonder if I'm just confused. My brain too cold to work properly.

Yutu sweeps the snow away from one corner with his foot.

'A bear has been here,' he says. 'Broke the door.'

A bear? Perhaps I am dreaming this. I want to ask if it's safe, but my mouth seems to be all frozen up too.

Yutu puts me down gently, propped up against the wall. He disappears for a few minutes, then returns with an armful of things from the snowmobile. I feel my eyes closing.

'Bea! Stay awake,' he says.

I watch. Unable to help. All my energy is concentrated on keeping my eyes open. He gets out the survival blanket.

'Try to sit up,' he says. Then he carefully leans me forwards and wraps the silver blanket in a cocoon around me. He unfolds a caribou skin and lays a sleeping bag on top. He helps me to wriggle my feet and legs inside, still wrapped in the survival blanket. He crouches down opposite me. I try to focus on his face in the gloom. I can see his eyes shining. Looking into mine with concern.

'Can you clench your hands into fists, then your toes, then your hands?' he asks. 'Keep doing it while I light the stove. I'm going to make a hot drink.'

I try to clench my fingers, but they feel stiff and weak. I can't feel my toes properly. I watch Yutu set up the stove, then gather two large pieces of wood from the floor. He leans them across the doorway, almost filling the gap.

I hear him say something under his breath as he rummages through one of the bags. He turns on the lantern torch and a soft light fills the room. He mixes something in a cup, then walks over to me. My arms are wrapped in several layers. He lifts the cup to my lips and tips it slowly. I drink a little bit. It's warm and slightly salty. He pauses, then lifts the cup again, until I've drunk it all.

'We should have stopped earlier,' he says. 'I'm sorry.'

I concentrate on clenching my frozen fingers and toes.

He comes back with another cup, steam billowing out. As I sip, there is a flicker of warmth in my stomach, but my feet and hands are still numb.

I remember doing the same things for Yutu after he'd fallen through the sea ice.

'Do I have hypothermia?' I try to ask, but my frozen face makes the words sound slurred.

Yutu seems to understand anyway. 'You have hypothermia, but not badly. It's my fault.'

He gently lifts one more cupful of soup to my lips.

'Are you starting to feel better?' In the lantern torchlight glow, I can see that his eyes are smiling.

I nod. 'Now I feel cold. Before I couldn't feel anything.'

'That's a start.' He scoops some snow from the opposite corner of the cabin and puts it in a small pan above the stove.

My eyes are drawn to the broken doorway beyond. 'Did you say something about bears?'

Yutu puts a lid on the pan and looks up.

'Yes. They break into cabins looking for food. They have less to eat,' says Yutu. 'The sea ice melts much earlier than it used to and so it's harder for them to hunt seals. They often go closer to villages and towns.'

With a shock, I realize he is talking about polar bears. A polar bear smashed in the door to this hut looking for food.

'Might it come back?' I ask quietly.

He looks around. 'There's a lot of snow inside the cabin, so there's probably been no door for a couple of days. It will have gone back to its lair. But if it smells food, it might return. Bears can cover big distances. We will need to stay awake tonight.'

'To listen for the bear?'

'To listen for the bear and because it's going to get a lot colder. There's no cloud cover. It's not a good night to have a hole in the door. It will be much warmer in here than outside though.'

He carries a few armfuls of snow from the opposite corner of the cabin and packs them in front of the makeshift door, then wedges another piece of wood on top. Now only a narrow strip of sky is visible.

He turns off the stove and joins me on the caribou rug, with a mug of tea. I look down to see the remains of my soup frozen solid in the cup.

He sips slowly, tearing off pieces of bread to eat.

Yutu doesn't seem to mind if we don't speak. Stella and her friends would fill every silence with whispers and giggles. Conversations were different too. Not comfortable and relaxed. More like quicksand, drawing you in only to suck you under. Innocent questions would trap you, compliments weren't really compliments.

'I guess we're even now,' I say after a few minutes.

Yutu tilts his head. 'Even for what?'

'Rescuing each other from hypothermia.'

He chuckles.

'It will be easy for us to end up like that again tonight if we are not careful. We have to get you to your mum in one piece.'

'Preferably not frozen.'

I try to imagine what Mum would think if she could see me now, in a snowy cabin in the Arctic, wrapped in emergency blankets and caribou skin.

'You said that you travel a lot with your family,' says Yutu. 'That sounds amazing. I've never really left my village.'

The kids at school always ask where I've moved from, then they want to know where else I've been. It's never long before they lose interest or start to think that I'm bragging.

'You eat a lot of aeroplane food and spend a lot of time packing,' I say.

Yutu nods. He's waiting for more.

'We have lived in lots of different places. Near deserts, in the mountains, in a few big cities.'

'Wow,' says Yutu, sounding impressed. 'You must have seen so much.'

'I guess so.' I pause. 'I actually wish we didn't move around so much.' I sense Yutu watching me. 'I just start to get used to a place and then we leave again.'

'How long do you normally stay?'

'About a year, sometimes a bit longer.'

'Do you pack all your stuff up every time you move?'

'Mum has a military-style system. She has spread-sheets for every room. They're colour-coded.' Now I've started talking I don't seem able to stop.

'What about your friends? Can you go back to visit them much? You must know people in so many countries.'

I'm about to say that I do, and it's hard to fit them all in. But I hear myself saying something else entirely.

'I don't really have any friends.' The words seem to hover around me.

Yutu doesn't react. Maybe he isn't surprised.

'I did have a best friend when I was little. We played together all the time. Her name was Alex. I was heartbroken when we moved away, but I made another best friend. The next time we moved it was even worse. We sent messages to each other for a while, but eventually she stopped writing.' I pull the caribou skin up closer to my chin. 'At the school I'm at now, some people actually seem to hate me. I've only been there four weeks.'

'I'm sorry to hear that,' says Yutu. 'Did something happen?'

'Not really.' I think for a bit. 'I guess I didn't try all that hard.'

'I've had the same friends since I was born. I've never had to try and make new ones.'

'Lucky you. It must be amazing to have friends who know everything about you.'

'I guess so. I've never really thought about it. They have just always been there.' He is silent for a bit, then he says, 'I do think about leaving. I think about living somewhere else. I think about it all the time. I can't imagine being without Grandma or my friends, or not seeing them every day. But we're not exactly into the same stuff. Maybe it's just me, I'm the odd one out and I'd be the odd one out somewhere else, too. But if I stay in my village, I'll never know.'

It's the longest I've ever heard Yutu speak in one go. He is still looking at me. Then he turns to stare through the gap at the top of the doorway for a while.

'Isn't there anyone you could be friends with?'

I think about the jar of honey in my locker. 'Maybe,' I say quietly.

Prey

I open my eyes. I'm not sure what woke me. I hear the gentle swish of wind. I see the snow on the ground and a faint strip of light at the top of the doorway and remember where I am.

Yutu is next to me, under the caribou skin. His shoulder is level with my ear.

'Bea, don't move.' He whispers so softly that his voice almost blends with the wind. 'There's something outside.'

My blood runs cold.

I strain to hear a noise through the walls, hardly daring to breathe.

There is a snuffling sound. Moments later I hear the crump of snow compressed as something heavy walks across it, then bumps against the side of the hut. I feel the wall vibrate. I want to look at Yutu, but daren't move. I take shallow breaths, trying not to let the sleeping bag rustle. I am aware that

Yutu is moving, slowly, soundlessly. His body is no longer touching mine. The soft crumping sound starts again. I hear sniffing. It's right in front of us, by the door. The planks move as something nudges against them.

In a split second Yutu leaps up, shouting, and shining his halogen torch at the gap in the door. I hear a grunting noise outside. Yutu carries on yelling.

There are thuds on the ground next to the hut, then silence.

I feel a flutter in my chest as Yutu goes right up to the door and shines his torch outside. After a few minutes he comes to sit down on the caribou skin.

Neither of us speaks. Once more the only sound is the wind.

I turn to look at Yutu. He is staring at the doorway, motionless. His face sculpted by the torchlight.

He seems to remember I am there.

'So the bear came back for another look,' he says quietly, still looking towards the door.

My heart thumps a little faster again.

'Do you think it's nearby?'

'I don't know. It wasn't expecting a nasty, noisy bright light. We just have to hope it's not desperate enough to try again. It might feel braver second time round.'

Yutu goes over to the bags and takes something from a side pocket. 'If it does come back, shine this and make as much noise as you can,' he says, passing me a torch.

I switch the torch on and off. It's like the one Dad bought me for our hiking trips as my emergency flashlight. I bet he never imagined me in this kind of emergency. I feel an ache in my chest as I think about how much I want to speak to him. To tell him what's happened. To see his face alive with surprise, with pride, with amazement, when he hears about our journey.

A warm tear rolls down my cheek, leaving an icy trail in its wake.

'I'm sorry I fell asleep,' I say, turning to look at Yutu. 'I know we both need to stay alert.'

He's sitting very still, staring through the gap at the top of the doorway, a faint smile on his lips. For a second, I wonder if he's actually frozen, like the soup.

I follow his gaze, and gasp.

Beyond the doorway, the sky is dancing. Greenish ribbons of flickering, whirling light illuminate the night.

'Aurora borealis,' says Yutu softly. 'The Northern Lights. You often see them on clear nights.'

'It's beautiful,' I whisper. 'Like Mother Nature is playing while people sleep.'

'Or the spirits of those who have died, playing a ball game with a walrus's head as the ball.'

I look at Yutu. 'What?'

'That's the story people tell here. It's the legend.' He chuckles softly. 'I didn't think it sounded strange until just now. We have stories for everything in nature. They're a good way to pass the time in winter.'

'I want to hear more of them,' I say.

'OK,' he says. 'But in return, you have to tell me some too.'

I think about 'Goldilocks and the Three Bears' or 'Puss in Boots'. Maybe the stories I grew up with sound weird too.

I am going to make it through the Arctic night like Yutu's ancestors. By sharing stories.

Dawn

My eyes are drawn once more to the gap at the top of the doorframe. Perhaps it's my imagination, but the oblong of sky seems a shade lighter. Yutu follows my gaze.

'Sunrise. You noticed before I did. Nature is claiming you back,' he says. 'Let's have something to eat. Then we should leave. A hungry bear might find it hard to resist the smell of seal soup again.'

'And maybe Miki wasn't able to convince everyone to start searching in the opposite direction,' I add darkly. 'Someone might have picked up our trail.'

Yutu nods and sets up the stove in a dry patch on the floor.

For the first time since we arrived, I ease myself out of the sleeping bag and pull on my snow boots. I stamp my feet and jump up and down a few times, trying to get my blood circulating.

'Letting the bear know it's breakfast time?' Yutu smiles, poking a frozen lump in the saucepan.

I roll up the sleeping bag and blankets and stuff everything back into the bag. Yutu passes me a cup of soup and some bread.

While I dip the bread and eat, I feel a flutter in my stomach as I think of the journey ahead, and whether we are being followed, or there's someone waiting for us at the other end. Getting closer to home makes me more nervous that something might go wrong. Anything seems possible after what happened to Dad.

Yutu packs up the stove and then places something in the corner of the room, on a piece of paper which had been wrapped around the bread. It's the mittens.

'It doesn't really make up for having your cabin ripped up by a bear, but Grandma would still want me to leave them.'

I hadn't thought about the owner of the cabin, and how hard it might be to fix up a cabin, miles from the nearest town.

'It's going to be very cold until the sun makes it over the horizon,' says Yutu. 'But I'll be going slowly until the light is better, which should help a bit.'

He tugs at the board covering the top of the door-way. It's frozen to the walls of the hut and comes away with a loud pop. The second board is wedged deep in the snow he piled up last night. I rush over to help. It's hard to get a good grip through my sealskin mittens, but with both of us pulling, the second plank comes away.

As we step outside, icy air steals my breath away. It was so much warmer in the cabin, despite the snow.

I push my hood back a little and scan the horizon, like Yutu does. The sky glows pinkish orange. In the pale light, the snowy landscape is a thundery grey mass. The wind whispers and a gentle rhythmic creaking sound rises up from the sea ice in the bay. Otherwise there is silence. It's beautiful. Dad would love it here.

I spot Yutu bending down near the back of the snowmobile and realize that the bear might have damaged it.

I walk over to see what he's looking at.

Pressed deep into the snow, next to one of the skis, is an enormous paw print. I could fit both my hands inside the dip.

'We were lucky,' says Yutu. 'It was a big bear.' He straightens up and looks over at the hills behind the hut.

I have a strange sensation of what it might feel like to be prey. A bear could be watching us, waiting for the moment to attack. Even a snowmobile couldn't outrun a bear over bumpy ground.

'Let's go,' says Yutu.

He turns the ignition and the engine revs with an explosion of sound to shatter the peace.

Melt

Our track snakes along the edge of a shallow hill. It's smoother than the rest of the route so far. Perhaps well-used by whoever owns the cabin.

A fiery strip of orange creeps above the horizon. The thundery grey hills turn pale yellow. I marvel at how I used to think the Arctic was white.

The snowmobile begins to slow and Yutu points to something up ahead. There are two peaks, higher than the others.

'We are almost there!' I shout.

Instinctively I turn to look at the route behind, but I see no dark shape. No one following us.

We race through the snow and I realize I'm enjoying the speed. My muscles ache less, and we haven't been on the move long enough for me to feel really cold.

We glide down a hill, gathering momentum. Yutu steers left to avoid some rocks at the bottom. When we are almost level with them, I realize something is wrong. He tries to slow down but we skid from side to side. Instead of pressing harder on the brakes, he accelerates again. There is a cracking sound. The skis hiss like we're driving through slush. I look again at the rocks and realize they aren't rocks at all. They are dark patches of water. We're crossing a river which has begun to thaw. The right-hand ski is partially submerged. The engine is whining at full revs but we're losing speed as the ice softens beneath us.

Yutu drives us forwards, leaning to the left so there is less weight on the right-hand ski. All it would take is one big crack beneath the machine and it would go under, pulling us with it.

The right side of the snowmobile drops down and I breathe in sharply, but there is enough traction at the front to pull us clear of the slush. We are almost at the opposite bank, where the ground rises steeply. I cling to Yutu, leaning left or right when he does.

We go over a big bump and the whine of the engine drops to a deeper sound. The skis are on solid ground again, but the added grip propels us forwards too fast. We spin to the right. Yutu turns left to try and straighten up but we keep on spinning. There is a loud crunching noise and the snowmobile jerks to a stop. Yutu lurches onto the handlebars at the front as I tumble onto the snow.

A few seconds pass. All I can hear is my breathing, fast and shallow, amplified within my hood. My knee hurts, and my thigh, from when I fell before. Yutu is silent. I push my hood back and look up at the snowmobile. He is slumped across the front of the machine.

I get to my feet and take a few deep breaths. I kneel in the snow and gently lift his hood. His eyes are closed. I try to stay calm. I shouldn't move him in case he's damaged his back or neck, but I can't leave him like this for long. While I am staring at his face, trying to work out what to do, his eyelids flutter. He opens his eyes, and looks at me, sunlight reflecting golden brown in his eyes.

'Does anything hurt?' I ask.

He blinks, then pushes himself up from the handlebars. 'My chest,' he says. He rubs his hand across his ribs and winces. 'Lucky I'm wearing so much padding.'

I sit down again in the snow. 'I thought you might be badly hurt,' I say. Tears pool in my eyes.

Yutu climbs down carefully from the snowmobile, which is leaning on one side. He crouches next to me.

'I'm OK. Just a bit sore.' He smiles. 'I can't say the same for the snowmobile.'

I look up to see what he means. The right-hand ski is broken.

'Can we fix it?' I ask, already knowing the answer.

'We're going to have to walk the last bit.'

'What about the snowmobile?'

'We have to leave it here. We don't have any choice. I'm sorry. We'll need to move quickly. It's not a good idea to be on foot after dark. There are more bears closer to town.'

Near

I let my feet find a natural rhythm. The bag of clothes and food is slung across my chest, thumping on my back with every step. It was too painful for Yutu to carry it.

We've been walking for a couple of hours. I try not to think about how far is left. The sun has passed its zenith and sparkles across the near side of the mountains, casting the far side into cold shadow.

If someone has decided to follow us, this will give them a chance to catch up. I keep glancing behind, but there is no sign of figures in the distance. I wonder what they might be planning instead.

Yutu is quiet. I can tell that he is in pain. He's not moving with his usual steady gait. When we stop to melt snow on the stove, he doesn't sit down. It puts too much pressure on his bruised ribs.

For the last thirty minutes or so we've been climbing steadily. My knee is beginning to throb. Low hills rise gently on either side. We enter a natural passageway between them. Its snowy sides deaden the sound of our footfall.

When the hills begin to flatten out again, I gasp. Below, to our left, the bay stretches as far as I can see. The sea ice here has melted to create a jigsaw of white and deep blue water. A kilometre to our right, a huge grey warehouse sits behind a jumble of square buildings in pastel colours. There is no road leading into town, but snaking along one side is a rail track.

I turn to look at Yutu. 'Is this where we're heading?'

He looks at me and smiles. 'Do you see any other towns around here?'

It's much bigger than Yutu's village, but tiny compared to where I live. Freight trains rest in orderly lines, near a station building. The rail track doesn't continue on the other side. This is the end of the line. In the other direction, lies home.

Parting

The snowy track becomes a yellowish gravel path which turns into a wide road running through the centre of town. I step on tarmac for the first time in almost a week. Instead of familiar, it feels weird. It's not actual ground, but several layers on top. I'd never realized how much of my world is covered in tarmac and concrete, and how rarely my feet are on real earth.

Yutu is still quiet. I'm not sure it's just the pain in his ribs now.

The town is no more than four or five rows of houses, either side of the main road. It's easy to find the station building. It's closed. To the right of the door is a buzzer to press. After a few minutes a woman appears round the side.

'Sleeper train?' she calls.

I look at Yutu. He nods. 'That's the only one which will take you all the way home.'

'Can I get a ticket for today?'

'Sure,' the woman says. 'You're lucky. It only runs three days a week.'

Yutu reaches inside his coat for the sealskin wallet.

'Thank you,' I say. 'You know I will make sure you get the money back, don't you?'

'I know,' says Yutu, his eyes twinkling at me through dark lashes.

'It doesn't leave for another three hours,' the lady says, 'but it's due to arrive soon. I'll let you on after the passengers disembark. You can wait in here,' she adds, unlocking a pale blue door. Inside is a small room with chairs around the edge. She switches on a heater halfway up the wall.

Yutu lowers himself gently onto one of the chairs.

'I'll stay with you until the train arrives,' he says.

'What will you do then?' I feel bad that during the whole journey I hadn't once thought about Yutu having to make the whole journey back again, alone.

'Grandma has friends here. They will be surprised to see me.'

'Surprised in a good way?' I ask.

'Of course,' he chuckles.

'What will happen to the snowmobile?'

'I think it just needs a new runner. Snowmobile parts aren't hard to come by. I'm hoping Grandma's friends will help me. They'll know a better route back.

One which doesn't go through the river. Grandma will feed them well at the other end.'

We are both silent for a while. For the first time, it feels awkward.

Then the silence is broken by a gentle rumbling noise outside. I look at Yutu, frowning.

'It's the tracks,' he says. 'Your train's coming.' He fiddles with the zip on the bag. 'Bea, can you give me your email address or a phone number?' He pauses. 'So that I can check you've made it back home OK?'

'Yes, and can I have yours too?'

Yutu smiles. 'I'll ask the stationmaster for a pen. Your emergency kit had everything except a pen.'

He goes outside to look for the woman, returning a few minutes later with a scrap of paper and a pen.

He gives me his grandmother's phone number. 'Sometimes the connection isn't great,' he says. 'You might need to keep trying.'

I put the piece of paper carefully in my pocket.

'Why don't you keep the bag?' I say. 'The emergency stuff might be useful, and a set of dry clothes.'

'OK. But take some food. I think it's a long journey.'

'Deal,' I say, just as the door to the waiting room opens. It's the stationmaster.

'You can get on if you want. It's warmer on the train.'

I stand up. 'It's not due to leave for a couple of hours. You should go before it gets dark.'

Yutu nods.

As I walk through the train to find my seat, he follows me, along the platform.

I sit down, and he raises a mittened hand in the air. I wave back. Then he puts his hood up and heads towards the street.

I watch until he fades from view.

The train lurches from the station and grinds slowly down the tracks, past a few buildings. In less than a minute I have left the town behind me. My eyes adjust to the vast horizon. White tundra sprawls for almost as far as the eye can see, rising into shadowy peaks. I want to ask Yutu what they're called. I look at the empty seat opposite. It feels strange to be on my own.

I take a deep breath and let it out slowly. I start to think about how close I am to discovering the truth about Dad, but the motion of the train feels so smooth, after days on the snowmobile. My eyelids are heavy. It's almost forty-eight hours since the last time I really slept. I pull a lever at the side of the chair. As the seat tilts back, a footrest rises up.

I don't want, *You look tired out, darling,* to be the first thing Mum says when I see her. After a few seconds I realize that's exactly what I want her to say. Before she puts her arms around me and gives me a hug.

Home

The train jerks a little from side to side. I open my eyes. It feels like I've been asleep for ages but it's still dark outside. I have no idea what time it is.

The carriage is quiet, except for a few gentle snores. I'm sharing it with two or three other people.

I try to work out which day it is. This must be the fourth night since I left home, so tomorrow is Wednesday. I wonder what Stella and the gang think has happened to me. Maybe that I'm ill, or just couldn't face going in to school. None of them could ever guess the real answer.

The last four days are tangled up in my head. I need to get my thoughts in order, to make sure I don't forget something, that I don't leave out any important detail about what happened to Dad. I try to picture the faces of the men who attacked him. I remember their surprise when I appeared at the window, the looks of determination when they came after me. Already their features seem less distinct. Could I pick them out in a crowd? I think about sprinting down the runway. How desperate they were to stop me from getting away. They didn't expect me to be there. A witness.

A flare of anger heats my chest when I think about the message they sent to Yutu's village. How dare they spread lies about Dad. It made me see how easy it is to believe things about people you've never met. Especially bad things.

I try to imagine I'm lying on my bed at home, looking up at the ceiling. That's where I go when I need to think. I imagine the soft padding of Hester's paws across the carpet. The little *miaow* as she jumps up to join me, walking in circles until she has just the right spot to lie down. Then I find myself thinking about Yutu, sitting on the little stool in Miki's house. The smell of bread mixed with pinewood.

The sky is turning a pale dawn-grey. A few houses are scattered in the distance. Everything looks dull and ordinary without a magical dusting of snow.

There is a crackling sound, then a muffled voice filters over the tannoy. We're due to arrive in fifteen minutes.

I feel a flutter in my stomach. I'm so close to home. Then with a shudder I remember that someone might be keeping watch, looking for me. I'll keep my hood up. It will be cold outside, so that won't seem strange. I don't have any bags, so maybe it won't look like I've just arrived. Another thought strikes me. I don't have any money for a taxi and I have no idea how to get home.

Almost imperceptibly the train begins to slow. There is a rustle of bags as people start to pack things away.

I slip my coat on, feeling the soft fur of my sealskin mittens in the pockets.

The brakes screech gently. I've never seen this station before. It doesn't feel like coming home, but it's bringing me back to Mum.

I pull up my hood and step into the morning air. It feels fresh on my face but doesn't snatch my breath away like on the tundra.

I scan the ticket hall. The exit is directly opposite. People hurry past to buy tickets or make their way to the platforms. I weave round them, moving quickly without seeming to rush. A man sits on a bench, reading a book. I notice him because he is still, within all the movement. It's impossible to know whether he's watching me too.

I turn right outside the station. It seems the busiest route. I keep walking until I see a sign to the town centre. I can find my way back from there. My legs ache from walking in the snow yesterday, but I pick up my pace. Every step is taking me closer to Mum. Closer to the truth. So far I have only been able to guess at what happened to Dad. At least with guessing, there are different possibilities.

The centre of town is humming with cars and people, everyone rushing to work or school. I'm beginning to sweat but I don't want to take my hood down, in case someone is following me.

After a few wrong turns, I'm on the wide avenue close to home. I turn left onto my street. There is a black car parked in the road. Everyone has their own drive. My heart starts to beat faster. It's too late to turn back. The car is sleek and expensive-looking. As I approach my house, I glance up, but keep walking, past the car, my head down like I'm lost in thought. At the end of my street I turn left, and then left again down a dirt path which runs between the back gardens.

I know that the sixth house on the left is mine. Halfway along our fence I see a gate. I twist the latch, but the gate doesn't budge. It must be bolted on the inside. I look around to see if anyone's about, then grasp the top of the fence and haul myself over, protected from the rough wood by my thick coat. I look up at the back of the house and pause for a minute. I can't see any movement inside.

I cross the grass to the back door and peer through the window. After a few minutes, I knock gently on the glass. No one comes. I knock again, more loudly. What if Mum isn't here? Then I see her, walking through the kitchen, her face is pale. She looks towards the back door, frowning. Then her eyes open wide, and her jaw drops a little. She grabs the key from the hook and fumbles to open the door. I throw my arms around her and bury my face in her shoulder. I stay there until Mum unwraps her arms and looks at me properly.

'Are you OK?' she says. 'That's all I need to know right now.'

I wipe my eyes on a soft mitten and nod.

'Then come and sit down.' She takes my hand and leads me to the kitchen table. 'I need to hear everything. Are you hungry?'

I should be hungry, but I don't feel like eating right now.

Mum reads my expression. 'Hot chocolate then?'

I nod again. All the things I planned to say seem to have evaporated. Hester pads into the kitchen. She sees me and gives a little *miaow* before running over, tail in the air.

Mum goes to the kitchen counter, but instead of picking up some mugs, she reaches for her phone and a scrap of paper and begins dialling a number. I leap up from my chair.

'Mum, stop!'

She looks up in surprise. 'What is it?' Then she sees me staring at the phone in her hand. 'I need to let people know you're safe. They are out looking for you.'

'Mum,' I say more quietly, 'can I talk to you first?'

She hesitates. 'OK. Perhaps that's a good idea.'

She puts her phone down.

When we're both sitting at the table with a steaming mug of hot chocolate, Mum says, 'Why didn't you call back? Bea, after you hung up, I had no idea where you were or if you were on your way home. Where have you been?'

I look at the dark circles underneath her eyes.

'I'm sorry,' I say. 'I didn't know what else to do. I wanted to talk to you, and when that man took your phone, I realized you weren't alone. I didn't want anyone else listening to what I had to tell you.'

'But they were trying to help,' says Mum.

'I have to talk to you about Dad.'

Mum pauses. 'Yes,' she says softly. 'We need to talk about Dad.' Mum is looking at me intently.

I realize that my ordered thoughts are competing to arrive at once, in a swirling, confusing rush. I need to calm down.

'Mum, when Dad and I landed in the Arctic, there were two men waiting for him at the airport. They attacked him. They didn't know I was there, but I saw it happen. I was looking through the window. Dad was lying on the floor. Then one of the men spotted me. He chased after me.' I realize I haven't really taken a breath. I feel a bit lightheaded. Mum is still watching me closely. 'I ran to the plane to get away, but he carried on chasing me, even when I was driving the plane along the runway.'

Mum takes my hand.

'I'm sure if I hadn't been there they would have— they might have—' I feel a sob rising in my chest. Mum walks round the table and pulls me into a hug.

'It's OK,' she says. 'You're here now.'

'But where is Dad?'

'Do you want to finish telling me first?'

I nod.

I tell her about how I flew the plane, alone, and landed it.

Mum shakes her head slowly and closes her eyes, but she doesn't look angry.

'I didn't crash into the hut though, which was lucky, because there was a boy inside it.'

'A boy?' Mum says.

'Yes. He had hypothermia. I gave him some dry clothes—some of Dad's, and some food. When he felt better, he drove me back to his village.'

Mum has stopped shaking her head, but her mouth is slightly open. 'So, this boy had a car?'

'No. There are no roads up there. He had a snowmobile.'

Mum closes her eyes and nods. 'Of course,' she says so quietly I can hardly hear.

I describe the warning message sent to the mayor.

'They were pretending to be the police. They didn't want anyone to speak to me. They didn't want anyone to know the truth. They tried to make it sound like I'd be really confused, that what I said couldn't be trusted.'

Mum is looking at me. Her expression isn't one of shock or horror at what I've just said. She doesn't even look surprised. The energy has gone from her eyes. I want her to say something. She isn't reacting in the way I thought she would. I want to know what she's thinking. I want to know what's wrong. I want to know what's happened to Dad.

'Dad's missing,' Mum says. A coldness creeps down my spine. What does *missing* mean?

Mum looks so tired. 'Bea,' she says slowly, 'there's no reason to think the people who left the message were pretending to be police.'

I scan Mum's face to check that she's serious. Her expression is unchanged.

'Dad has done something he shouldn't have done,' she says.

'No,' I say, shaking my head.

'Bea, when you flew north with Dad, he had arranged to meet someone.'

'Yes, they were going to take us to our hotel, or wherever we were supposed to be staying that night.'

'No,' Mum says quietly. 'Dad had arranged to meet someone he could give a file to. A file with secrets about the oil company. Secrets which he would get paid a lot for.'

I keep on shaking my head.

'Bea, Dad didn't need to fly north for a work trip. They hadn't asked him to do a survey there.' Mum takes a deep breath in and lets it out slowly. 'He was going to sell information. It's called industrial espionage.'

'They're lying. I saw what happened. I was there. They attacked him. They took him by surprise. There were two of them—'

'Darling, I want to believe it too.' She closes her eyes.

'Then why don't you tell them it isn't true? Why don't you tell them what I saw?'

'Bea, the person Dad was selling the secrets to, had a change of heart. He knew it was risky. He got in touch with the company. He told them what Dad was doing. The company bosses said the meeting should go ahead as planned, and then they could catch Dad red-handed. That's what you saw. That's what happened. The detectives explained everything to me. They've been working on the case for several weeks.'

My head is spinning. I don't want any of what Mum is saying to be true, and yet it no longer feels impossible.

'So where is Dad now?'

'When they confronted him, he escaped. He's on the run. They say that someone else must have been helping him.'

We are both silent.

Hester prowls around my feet, annoyed that I'm not giving her any attention.

'I should have done something,' Mum says. 'Dad wasn't himself. I should have tried to find out what was wrong.'

I'm not used to Mum having doubts. She's always

so certain.

My head is a jumble of truth and lies. It feels like I'm seeing the last four days through some kind of kaleidoscope; with a simple twist, the story has changed shape completely. Dad must be innocent. That was the one fact I could trust. But Mum doesn't think so, and she's told me why. The company knew all about this before it even happened.

But Mum didn't see Dad running from the building, clutching his head, warning me I had to escape. She wasn't there. If she had been, she wouldn't think that Dad was caught red-handed. She would think he was attacked.

'What happens now?' I say, trying to stay calm.

'I'm not sure,' says Mum. 'I think they will formally charge him. Bea, there's something else you should know.'

Something in her voice makes me look up, even though I want to lay my head on my hands and go to sleep where I am, at the kitchen table.

'There have been reports in the newspapers about a local man and his daughter going missing. The company wants to keep the story as quiet as possible. They know it will be hard for us. Even so, if Dad is charged with espionage, and they get wind of you flying a plane on your own across the Arctic, then that's more of a story. Much more.'

'Is that why there's a car parked outside our house?'

Mum looks startled. 'Is there?' She gets up. 'I wonder if some journalists have got hold of our address,' she says, almost to herself.

'Mum—if you go to look, they might think something's happened.'

'Is that why you came through the back door? Because of the car outside the front?'

'I thought the men who attacked Dad might be waiting for me.'

A wave of tiredness makes me feel like I can barely sit up any more.

'Mum, I think I have to go to bed. Will you wait a bit longer before you call the police?'

Mum looks uncertain.

'Please. Just until tomorrow morning. I need a little bit of time to let everything sink in.'

'OK,' says Mum. 'But we call first thing in the morning.' I nod. 'Will you have something to eat first? It's lunchtime and you've only had a cup of hot chocolate.'

'I'll have a big breakfast when I wake up, I promise. I just really need to sleep.'

Mum hugs me again. 'I can't believe you're home,'

she murmurs into my hair.

Hester runs ahead of me, her tail in the air. She wants to get the best spot on the bed.

Midnight

A strip of moonlight glows through the curtains. I can't sleep while my mind is whirring. I try to picture Dad sleeping peacefully somewhere. But words like *espionage* and *custody* keep drifting into my head. How can they apply to my dad? Everything is so different to how I'd imagined on my journey home. Mum thinks there is nothing we can do. If the oil company says it knew about the deal, knows the man Dad had planned to meet, then the evidence is too convincing.

Hester's front paw twitches in her sleep.

If there have been reports in the local newspaper, then everyone at school will know about them. What will Stella do if she has some real material to use against me? Perhaps she'll come up with a new sound to make every time I walk past. Maybe a police siren. My stomach twists at the thought of going back.

The strip of moonlight ripples as a gentle breeze touches the curtain. I opened my window before climbing into bed. It's freezing outside but the air in the house feels stuffy.

Hester twitches again. That's what I was supposed to remember. *Tell Bea—Hester.* I push my covers away. Hester leaps off the bed in disgust. Hester can't help, but maybe I can.

Without turning my light on, I push my bedroom door open and pad softly down the stairs.

I walk silently through to the front room, towards the thick curtains. Without lifting the fabric, I peer through a crack at the side to the street, bathed in moonlit shades of grey. The black car is still parked in front of the house. There is at least one figure sitting in the front. There isn't enough light to make out their features, or whether they are dozing or awake.

I walk back through the sitting room, towards Dad's study. I push down gently on the door handle and step inside. I've only been in here a couple of times. It seems darker than the rest of the house. There is a smell of books and paper. I look around. There's a filing cabinet, some bookshelves and a desk. On the desk is a coaster, a pot full of pens, a small pad and a pencil. Nothing looks unusual or out of place. What should I be looking for? A few minutes ago,

I felt sure I would find some answers in here. Now I feel silly. I tug at the filing cabinet door, but it's locked. I pick up the pencil. Dad was the last person to hold it. The pad is a similar size to Dad's note. I pick up the pad too. I stand still for a moment and try to imagine Dad sitting behind his desk, looking up as I come in. I imagine him smiling, saying everything is going to be OK. But I know it's not.

As I pull the door closed behind me, something touches me gently on the shoulder. I spin round. It's Mum, wrapped up in her dressing gown, looking even paler in the moonlight. Instinctively I hide the pad and pencil behind my back.

Mum's voice is calm, 'Come on, darling. You should get back to bed. I heard a noise downstairs and came to investigate. I didn't mean to scare you.'

'Sorry. I just wanted to look in Dad's office. I'm not sure why.' I feel my cheeks flush and am grateful to be standing in shadow.

'Some officers are going to come and take the files away from Dad's office. Anything to do with work.'

I feel tears prickle in the corner of my eyes.

'They can't just come and take his stuff.'

'If it might contain evidence, then they can.'

'I'm going to go back to bed,' I say, hoping that tears don't start to fall before I make it to the stairs.

I don't want Mum to see me crying. I walk past her and run up to my room, Hester at my heels.

I sit on my bed and listen to Mum walking slowly back up to bed.

I realize that I'm angry with her. Perhaps I want her to prove the evidence was wrong, that somehow Dad must be innocent. I want her to fix things.

When I think Mum is safely back in bed, I take my laptop from my desk. I wait impatiently for it to power up.

Where should I start? I type in the name of Dad's company. They drill for oil all over this part of the world. There are images of people looking busy and of trees and countryside. The website doesn't show any massive refineries or pipes snaking their way through the landscape from drilling site to processing plant. I read everything but have no new ideas.

A feeling of desperation builds in my chest. I've discovered nothing useful and no one knows where Dad is. People will come to our house to start taking his things away. Journalists will write about him and school will be more unbearable than ever, and I will have to face it without Dad. What if the police want to go and talk to Yutu and Miki too?

I wish I could speak to Yutu now.

Puzzle

When I wake, light is streaming through the curtains. Why didn't I set an alarm? I tug a pile of clothes from my chair and pull out jeans and a T-shirt, then rush downstairs to the kitchen.

Mum is on the phone. A cold wave passes over me.

'Yes, that would be best,' she says, and puts the phone down. She turns to me and takes a deep breath. 'That was a journalist. I don't know how they got our private number.'

I feel myself relax a little. She hasn't called the police.

'I made you some pancakes,' she adds, smiling, but the smile doesn't reach her eyes.

The plate in the middle of the table is piled with too many pancakes for two people.

'Bea, it's time I told the police you are here. Perhaps we need to think of a reason for not calling yesterday.'

I put down the piece of pancake I'm holding. My mouth feels dry.

'Mum, did Dad say anything about Hester before we went away?'

She frowns. 'No, I don't think so. Why?'

'There was a note in his pocket. In the trousers he'd packed. It said *Tell Bea—Hester.*'

She puts her fingers to her lips in thought, then slowly shakes her head.

'I'm going to have a quick shower and think about what to say to the police. I won't be long.'

'OK,' she says. 'Half an hour.'

I stuff one more piece of pancake in my mouth and then run upstairs.

Instead of the shower, I go back to my room and pick up Dad's pad and pencil. Then lie on my bed and stare at the ceiling.

Hester is watching suspiciously from the chair. I put my hand out towards her.

'I promise not to push my bedcovers onto you again.' She stares at me for a few seconds more. Just to make sure it's clear who was in the wrong. Then she jumps across to the bed.

I scratch her between the ears. 'Are you keeping secrets from me?' I whisper. She rubs her head against my arm. I realize that her collar isn't making its soft tinkling noise any more. Perhaps the silver identity disc has fallen off. I wave the pencil above her head. She can't resist batting it with her paw. As she looks up, I see the disc is missing, but there is something in its place. A small black oblong. I undo Hester's collar and slide it over the end. I stare into the palm of my hand. The oblong is a USB stick.

I roll over onto my stomach and plug the stick into my laptop.

'Bea!' Mum shouts from the hall.

'Just a minute!' I call back. My laptop whirrs but nothing happens.

Mum's footsteps thud softly up the stairs. As she enters my room, there is a loud knock at the front door.

'Bea,' she says more softly, 'I have to answer it.'

'I didn't know they'd be coming to get Dad's stuff so soon,' I say.

She turns to leave.

'Mum, wait!' I say to her back.

She turns around and closes her eyes. 'I don't want this to be happening either, but we could be charged with obstructing the course of justice.'

'There's something you need to see,' I say quietly. 'That note from Dad, *Tell Bea—Hester.*'

Mum frowns.

233

I show her the USB stick. 'This was on her collar.'

Mum sits on the edge of my bed. 'Why would Dad put it on Hester's collar?'

'We need to find out what's on there,' I say.

There's another knock at the door.

'You could be in the shower,' I say desperately. 'It's the morning. People have showers in the morning.' I can tell that Mum is wavering. 'What if they search the whole house for anything which might be evidence? They might take my laptop too.'

'Let's look,' she says, 'but quickly.'

A box has popped up on the screen. It says *Password*. I type in *Beatrice* but nothing happens, so I try *Hester*. Nothing. My palms are damp with sweat. I'm sure Dad wouldn't have made this difficult for me. I just need to think. Words fly around my head, but I know none of them are right. Mum is beside me, staring intently at the screen.

I feel like ripping the computer open or shaking it until the secrets fall out. It sits there, infuriatingly silent. There is another knock at the door. Someone shakes the handle.

Slowly, I begin to type again. *Wing Commander*. Nothing happens. I remove the space, *wingcommander*, and press enter. A list of files appears.

Mum gasps. 'That's it!'

My mouth feels dry as I click on the first file. As it opens, I see a document with lots of maps and graphs. My eyes scan the text, desperate to make sense of it. What did Dad want me to see?

After a few seconds, I realize that I know what this is. Dad has told me about geological surveys and seismic surveys and piecing together information for reports which show every important detail about a new drilling site. Some of them are top secret. If a rival company gets hold of one, they will know exactly what their competitor is planning. I've never seen one. Until now. But why would Dad want me to see it?

I open the next file. This one has Dad's name at the top. It includes some maps from the first file. I scroll through to the end.

'Go back a bit,' says Mum.

I scroll back to where it says *Summary* and begin to read. I don't understand all the technical words, but the meaning is clear. Oil can't be extracted without risk to the public. It won't be possible to get oil from this site.

The next file shows maps of a new area. It's a section of coastline. I can't work out why it looks strange, then I realize it's because there are no roads marked. There are hardly any towns either. I read a name at the southern end of the map. It sounds familiar, then I realize it's the town I went to with Yutu. The town where I caught the train. This map is a map of the Arctic.

'Why would an oil company be looking at maps of the Arctic?' I murmur to Mum.

There are two files left. I click on the one which says *Emails*.

They are between Dad and two people at his new company.

In the first, Dad says that extraction near the town isn't viable. In the next, he says his decision is final, he won't write a report to support their proposed new drilling site. Sea ice and storms make the risk of a large spill likely, which would be catastrophic for the region. There is a reply underneath. They hope Dad will reconsider his decision. Dad replies to say he will never support drilling in the Arctic. The next message says that Dad is an expensive member of the team, and this decision has grave implications for the company. It may also have implications for him. Three or four messages follow, then one which says they will give Dad another chance to comply, or else face serious consequences.

There is a final email. Separate from the others. The tone has changed. It's more friendly. It says the company will need further evidence from Dad, about why drilling would be 'catastrophic'. A plane and accommodation will be made available. The dates match when I travelled up with Dad. And the airport. Dad hadn't arranged to meet someone he could sell secrets to. The company had sent him.

'Oh no,' Mum gasps. 'He was set up.'

She puts her face in her hands.

'Because he wouldn't write the reports they needed?'

Mum looks at me. 'The men who came to see me weren't detectives,' she whispers.

There has been no sound from the front door for a few minutes. 'Mum,' I say, 'is the back door locked?'

She nods.

I click on the final file. It's a media file. There are no images, just a sound recording. One of the voices is Dad's. It's over so quickly that I don't hear what's being said. I click *play* again.

I hear Dad saying slowly, 'Hear you?' then a man's voice saying, 'We hope you make the right decision. Until you do, keep an eye on your daughter. You wouldn't want anything to happen to her.'

I realize I'm holding my breath.

I hear a thud and a scrabbling sound from the garden. I push my curtains aside. There is a man halfway over our back fence. Another man is waiting in the garden.

'I'm going to call the police.' Mum rushes to her bedroom to get the phone. 'The real police.'

Minutes later, the back door rattles. I'm not sure the police will get here in time. I have to make sure someone else knows about what's happened.

I type in the name of the local newspaper and scan down for contact details. There is an email address for the news desk. I copy and paste it. In the body of the email I write *Password: wingcommander*. I attach the files, then press *send*.

They wanted a story. Now they have one.

AFTER

AW 1

There is a knock at the front door. It makes me jump, even though I know there's nothing to be frightened of any more.

I hear Mum hurry across the hall, the click as she opens the door. Then silence. I run down the stairs to see her standing on the front step. Someone is hugging her. He looks up and smiles at me. A proper smile, like the ones he gave me before any of this started, and I know that Dad is back. Really back.

Mum puts on the kettle and we sit down at the table. It's almost as if nothing has happened. Then I look at the greenish-yellow bruise on the side of Dad's head. At Mum and Dad's pale, tired faces. Also, the phone won't stop ringing.

'I would have been back yesterday evening but the doctor wanted to observe me overnight, because of the blow to my head.' Dad puts his hand on top of mine.

We sit in silence for a moment. It feels so good to be together.

'I'm not sure how this would have turned out if you weren't so brilliant,' he says, 'escaping from those men, trekking across the Arctic tundra, then finding my files on Hester's collar.'

'Hester played her part brilliantly.'

The last few days have felt like endless interviews, questions and phone calls. First at the police station, then with journalists. Now that Dad is here next to me, I have questions of my own—even though the police did their best to answer most of them. But I know I have to wait. Dad has been held captive for almost a week. The police said he would need some time to adjust to what has happened to him. Some space.

Hester walks in to see what all the fuss is about, she trots straight past Dad and weaves herself around my legs.

'I guess not everyone in this house has missed me,' smiles Dad.

Over the next few days, we sleep, eat and talk about the things that happened while we were apart.

Dad tells us how he saved the files just before we left. He didn't think he'd need them, but if something did happen, it would be his word against the company's. About how after the phone call he didn't want to let me out of his sight. He thought while we were away, he could think of a way to fix things. That he wished he'd just gone to the police.

On the first warm day of spring, we sit in the garden together, enjoying the sunshine.

'Did this really all happen because you wouldn't write those reports?' I ask Dad.

He smiles. The bruise on the side of his head has nearly disappeared.

'Not writing those reports was a big deal. The company was paying me a lot of money and I wasn't going to make any for them. The new guy was ruining all their plans. Someone at the top decided to get me out of the way.'

'Do you think they were planning to get you out of the way'—I pause—'completely?'

Dad closes his eyes for a second.

'Perhaps. Maybe saying I was stealing company secrets was their plan B.'

He takes a sip of tea.

I think about the tea we took with us in a flask,

the day we flew to the Arctic. The tea which saved Yutu's life, so far from anyone else who could help.

'How did the police find you up there?' I ask.

'Once they'd caught the men trying to break into the house, I don't think it was very hard. They had nothing to lose by assisting the police, telling them where I was being held. Maybe even a reduced sentence for cooperating. They were only the middlemen after all. Someone at my company was the mastermind.'

'But why did they want to go ahead with the drilling near a town, if it wasn't safe?'

'Greed can do strange things to people.'

'I thought oil companies made loads of money.'

'But you can always make more. When I wouldn't agree to say it was safe, they brought forward a second plan, to drill in the Arctic. They had been relying on my reputation to create a convincing report. Something which might make the government change its mind and allow drilling there. But I wouldn't. A spill would destroy the wildlife and the communities there for ever.'

I think of Yutu. About how his village is already suffering.

'But you've worked in other beautiful places. Don't they get damaged too?'

Dad sighs. 'They do, Bea. Now the Arctic is one of the only wildernesses we have left. We can destroy that too, or we can say enough is enough. There are plenty of other jobs I could do. This one just paid the best.'

I feel a twist in my stomach. 'Does that mean we'll be moving again?'

'Mum and I need to talk about things.' He squeezes Mum's hand. 'But perhaps AW1 has just been brought forward.'

I feel a fizz of excitement in my stomach. 'Seriously!?' I say.

Dad looks at Mum for a reaction. She is staring at her hand in Dad's.

'I'm so sorry I believed them,' she says quietly, looking up at my dad. 'When those two men came to see me, they made it sound so real. Like there was no room for doubt about what you'd done.'

'You don't need to apologize. Even once. Definitely not the three hundred times you have since I've been back.' He smiles again. 'They were professionals,' Dad says. 'Criminals, yes, but professionals. It was their job to make you believe them.' He takes a deep breath. 'I think we've heard enough about me. Let's talk more about Yutu. I've been told that we should be very grateful to him for saving you after you'd crash-landed my plane in the tundra.'

'Yutu?' I say. I feel my cheeks burning. 'I saved him first.'

'Well,' says Dad, 'I would expect nothing less.'

I pull the crumpled piece of paper from my coat pocket and smooth it flat. I type in the number scrawled at the top. After a few seconds it starts to ring.

A voice at the other end says, '*Halu.*'

'Yutu? It's Bea.'

'Bea, I've been hoping you would call.'

Summer

Wind whips my hair in all directions. I sweep it from my face and stare across the water, searching for a smooth white shape within the waves. Seconds earlier I spotted my first beluga whale, its pale fin arcing above the water.

The boat pitches sharply and I grab the handrail, planting my feet a little further apart. I'm not used to the rolling motion of the waves. The floor vibrates gently with the low throb of the engine. I can smell diesel mixed with fresh air and seaweed.

A woman waves to me from the small cabin at the bow of the fishing boat. I am hitching a ride with old friends of Miki's. We don't have a plane we can borrow any more. They use too much fuel, anyway.

Mum and Dad travelled with me as far as the harbour. We made the same train journey I'd taken three months before only this time in reverse.

Dad wasn't keen for me to travel the rest of the way without them, but Mum pointed out that I'd already done it in sub-zero temperatures on a snowmobile, so a fishing boat with experienced sailors seemed fine. And no mercenaries were searching for me this time either. Since Dad came home, things are different with Mum. We talk more. Not so much about things I should or shouldn't do, but about things we like, or plans for the future.

I pull the newspaper page from my pocket. Yutu has read everything online, but there's something extra-special about seeing it in print. It describes Yutu driving me to safety, and how we escaped the bear, about me flying the plane and Miki sending the attackers on a wild goose chase.

When the story broke, students I'd never met before high-fived me in the corridors. Even Stella wanted to be friends, but we have different definitions of friendship. There are a few girls I hang out with at school now. Girls who like me when I'm just being myself.

I smile when I think back to my last visit to Yutu's house. So much has changed since then. Dad is setting up his adventure activity business. Mum has been studying. She used to work as a marine biologist before moving every year took up most of her time. She used to climb, too.

The boat has been following the coastline north. The hills rising up from the shore are soft shades of yellow and brown.

The noise of the engine changes as the boat turns gently inland. Several minutes later a scattering of houses appears from behind a low hill. As we get closer, I see a figure standing by a short pontoon. Yutu.

I clamber over the side of the boat and jump down, helped by Miki's friends, who can't be much younger than Miki.

They greet Yutu by pressing their noses against his forehead, then carry on walking up the pontoon. Yutu turns to me. It's strange to see him wearing just a T-shirt and jeans. His brown eyes twinkle, the corners of his mouth rise in a smile.

'Hello, Bea,' he says. 'Welcome back.'

I have so much to tell him, yet we barely say a word on the way to Miki's house. I just breathe in the salty air and feel myself relax into the endless space.

The door to their home is open. Miki comes out and hugs me. She seems even tinier than before.

I enter the warm peace of their home. I notice that the carvings and ornaments have gone. Miki sees me glancing around. She exchanges a look with Yutu.

'Is everything OK?' I say.

Miki sighs, then presses her fingertips to her eyes. Yutu leads her to a chair.

'What's the matter?' I ask.

'We have to leave,' says Yutu.

'Leave where?'

'Our home,' says Yutu.

'Why? What's happened?'

'Every year the temperature rises and the permafrost melts a little more. Now the houses in our village are beginning to collapse, including Grandma's. There is nothing solid to support them any more.'

'First the animals start to disappear, then the sea ice, now our home,' says Miki.

I try to picture Miki in one of the modern houses, with neat flat walls and front doors all the same shade of grey.

'Do you know which house you will move to?'

'There is nowhere in the village. Many people are having to move out, and these houses are some of the most expensive in the country. It's so hard to build here.'

I try to take in what Yutu is telling me. 'So you will have to move away, somewhere else?'

'Yes. It will be a big town, further south.'

Miki goes over to the stove. 'We can talk about this later,' she says. 'You must be hungry after your journey.'

After we've cleared up the dinner things and Miki is sewing in her chair. Yutu and I sit on the doorstep, bathed in the golden glow of the sun.

'It will only set for a couple of hours tonight,' he says. 'In winter it barely rises, in summer it barely sets.'

'Perhaps you can come and visit me next time,' I say. 'Miki could come too.'

'She doesn't really like to leave the village,' says Yutu, then closes his eyes when he realizes what he's said. 'I used to think that I would leave here at the first chance I got. But now I know that depended on me being able to come back. On my home always being here.'

I let his words sink in. It's what I've always wanted too. Somewhere to really call home.

'I know I've travelled around a lot,' I say, 'but you showed me how to look differently at what was right in front of me.'

Simple things, like enjoying silence, noticing the weather, the feel of the ground beneath my feet. Things I never even noticed before, because the bonds which connect people and nature are beginning to fray. Something precious beyond imagining, is coming apart. But it's not too late to change that.

Not yet.

Acknowledgements

This book was written (mostly) during lockdown. Everyone's worlds were turned upside down. Thank you to the many amazing friends who helped to turn ours the right way up again. Too many to list here, but special big-up to Phil Sawkins, the Fox Mums, and to Helena, Brian, Poppy and Livvy, for your encouragement, socially distanced visits, doorstep present deliveries, veg patch envy and help with nominators and denominators.

Thank you to the amazing teaching staff who helped our children and many others to navigate uncharted waters. Mr Vincent somehow managed do this with a newborn baby too.

Thanks to Charlie Viney as ever. Thank you to Sarah Odedina for your editing wisdom and brilliance, and to Adam Freudenheim and the dream team at Pushkin Children's Books: India, Rory, Poppy, Elise, Natalie, Kirsten. Thank you to Thy for the beautiful cover, and to Hannah for tidying me up.

Thank you to the children's authors whom I admire and learn from daily, and to the booksellers, librarians and reviewers who champion children's books through thick and thin, and also through pandemics.

Thank you to Mum and Dad always, and to Judy for your support and common sense.

Thank you to Tim, Lily and Scarlet, for making home schooling and home working possible. We will never forget Pizza Wednesday, Joe Wicks (or nominators and denominators). Although we frequently forgot which day of the week it was. You are entirely magnificent.